EMAILS TO RAIL

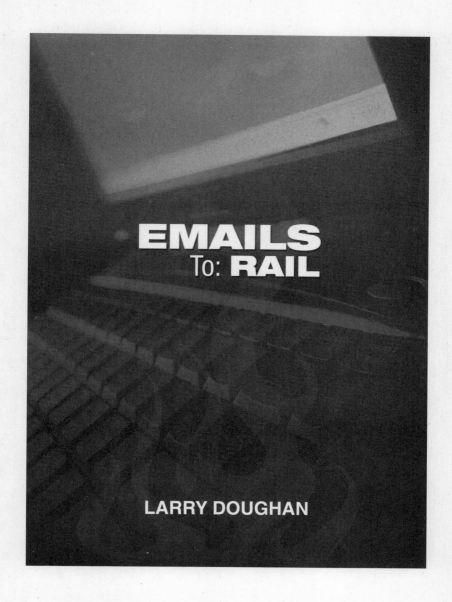

EMAILS To: RAIL

LARRY DOUGHAN

HighWay
A division of Anomalos Publishing House
Crane 65633

HighWay
A division of Anomalos Publishing House, Crane 65633
© 2008 by Larry Doughan
All rights reserved. Published 2008
Printed in the United States of America
08   1
ISBN-10: 0978845390 (paper)
EAN-13: 9780978845391 (paper)

Cover illustration and design by Steve Warner
Scripture taken from THE MESSAGE, Copyright © 1993, 1994, 1995,
1996, 2000, 2001, 2002. Used by permission of NavPress Publishing
Group.

A CIP catalog record for this book is available from the Library of
Congress.

Through the many months of finishing this work,
I recognized again that God had given me an incredible gift:
a wife who carefully listens, critiques, and encourages me.
Thank you, Connie.

Introduction

YEARS AGO, as I began to walk with the Lord, He harnessed several of the works of C. S. Lewis, using them to encourage and challenge me to think carefully about the implications of following Christ day by day. Second to God's Word, the single book that appeared to illustrate and apply His Word to our culture most effectively was *The Screwtape Letters.*[1]

Over the years, our culture has changed but Satan has not. He is still deceptive, power-hungry, and seeks to snatch as many as he can, making slaves of all whom he can dupe into not trusting Christ.

I am thankful to the Lord for the writings of C. S. Lewis that challenge me to think carefully. I offer you the same opportunity. In the pages that follow, you will find numerous emails that seem to have arrived at my email address by mistake. Perhaps there was a single letter misplaced in the email address, or some other electronic tangle. Regardless of the cause, in each case, the communication was clearly meant only for the regional demon-in-training, Rail (Liar). They had been sent by another of Satan's army, whose post might best be described as Rail's director, manager, or superintendent, and whose job description appears to include the task of overcoming and belittling all that would receive his communication. Thus the e-name: Slave Maker. As I considered the issues these emails appeared to raise, I often forwarded them to friends to receive their input and from time to time, shared them in a chat room online.

Most of the responses I have attached at the end of each addressed to Rail come from six friends: Colin, Adam, Ryan, Corinne, Kim, and Katie. Colin, Adam, and Ryan are three of the best friends I have ever had. They all love the Lord. Colin is an executive in a large corporation. He's sharp in the business world. It is plain that Colin understands how the demands and rewards of his career could tempt him to elevate it to the verge of becoming the god of his life. Adam wears many hats, involved with oversight of his construction company at one level and coaching at another. He coaches at the nearest high school because he loves sports and he loves kids. Ryan is the chief philosopher of my friends. When I begin to ponder the relevance of some part of life, the first guy I'm likely to call is Ryan.

All three are married. Colin married Corinne. She is the person most tuned-in to the drama of life. Adam and Kim are together too. Like her spouse, Kim was always involved in sports in her youth and still loves sporting events of almost every type. She understands what it means to have goals in life and strategies to reach those goals and invests a great deal of her time into their children. Ryan and Katie are the last couple. While Ryan is the philosopher of our group, Katie teaches in a nearby elementary school because she loves helping children. It is probably because of that love of youngsters that she never looks past what I too often dismiss as simple.

Due to the very nature of chat room anonymity, I do not truly know those who responded in that forum. Remember when you read their notes that Lilly, Jackson, Thatcher, and Harry are unknowns. Nonetheless, some of their observations may act as jumpstarts for your own consideration of the issues raised in this string of e-mails.

As you read, please remember that with occasional firewall blocks, system crashes, and software incompatibilities, email does not always come through clearly. In addition, remember that a lot of what floats around on the web is blatantly false.

While the existence of these emails is a charade, I do not doubt that they parallel some you have heard yourself. In response to the lies Satan uses as he seeks to deceive us, each email ends with a response from God's Word. In each case they are from *The Message*.[2]

As much as possible, I have included the quotes from His Word that you find at the end of each of these supposedly intercepted emails.

With that in mind, it is my hope that evalS rekaM's messages to Rail might provide useful snapshots of several of the avenues our enemy is traveling today as he persists, seeking to lure us to focus on anyone or anything other than Jesus Christ. As I continue to mull over the emails that have come my way, my reflection is drawn consistently to God's throne of grace.

Yours in His Grace Alone,

Larry

Email 1

FROM: evalS_rekaM@loweryet.net
TO: Rail@hellnet.com
Subject: Order and Rank
Received: 01.06.06

Rail,

Let me remind you that regardless of what others have told you, I am in command. You are not. I know your tech ability is low, but do not ever fool yourself. Mine is lower yet. I have seen your records and know you have tested at the extreme bottom of your class of dishonesty. Be that as it may, not one has ever tested as transcendently low as me—except perhaps for Larry L., David A., Timothy F., Connie M., Barbara A., Katherine T., Raymond A., and Lisa L. They have consistently tested lower than other humans. In addition, a few of all the graduates from 1956–2005 were proven to mark themselves somewhat lower than generations preceding them. Nonetheless, my relentless demotions have proven that I have mastered falsehood far more completely.

While often labeled technical disability, you and I both know that the weak-minded unreasonable, common lie is the instrument used most frequently. As time passes, you will learn that regardless of the unknown source, humans foolishly swallow virtually every email as though its existence in Internet land means it is without flaw and therefore comes to them completely trustworthy, loyal, helpful, courteous, kind, obedient, cheerful, thrifty, brave, clean, and reverent.

Nonetheless, be cautious in how you depend upon the use of such a tool. Never fool yourself into believing that I am not scrutinizing you 24/7.

evalS_rekaM :-{(

Responses I received:

FROM: Adam@anet.net
Our basketball team has months off between seasons. Yet with enemies at war 24/7, armies don't take a day off. I wonder why I have so often thought that one hour a week at spiritual work, you know, going to church, would be enough?

FROM: Ryan@rpie.com
How true. I eat everyday (my wife says way too much). Where did I ever get the idea that once a week would ever be all I need?

—

. . . God made a covenant with his people and ordered them, "Don't honor other gods: Don't worship them, don't serve them, don't offer sacrifices to them. Worship God, the God who delivered you from Egypt in great and personal power. Reverence and fear him. Worship him. Sacrifice to him. And only him! All the things he had written down for you, directing you in what to believe and how to behave—well, do them for as long as you live. And whatever you do, *don't worship other gods!* . . ."

2 KINGS 17:35–37

Email 2

FROM: evalS_rekaM@loweryet.net
TO: Rail@hellnet.com
Subject: Knowing What Tom Is Doing
Received: 01.13.06

Rail,

Let me pick up where I was interrupted in the midst of my last message. Do not delude yourself. You and I both know the Internet can be a useful tool in sowing lies anonymously. But it is not infallible. Keep changing the look in what you send or you will lose his attention.

Living proof is your own naiveté in believing that Tom swallows everything you send his way. The truth, disgusting as it is, is that Tom was so busy in the last 72 hours that he deleted all your e-mails without even opening them. He is busier than you think. Thus my most recent trainee, Re-Hack, labors to establish mail which opens itself upon reception, regardless of settings of the software on the recipient's computer and automatically downloads S.P.Y., our most recently developed invisible software.

While I am sure that you believe you are safe as you operate primarily on the web, let me point out to you once again that is not the case. Numerous devices are placed on the market each day, constantly seeking to protect those who dare to stand up against us. Nonetheless, with your new development of anti-non-glimpse software, you opened the door for Non-Anti-S.P.Y. the most recent piece developed by our CEO, Natas. In spite of that achievement, do not begin to pat yourself on the back. You are still far from genuinely accomplishing a thing with Tom.

The typical human of Tom's generation believes he or she is capable of handling a dozen projects at once and performing at a suitable level with every one of them. This foolhardy perception is due primarily to the efforts of Rail

#'s 1–3 and their previous labors to instill a self-centered, self-focused pride in their lives. The speed of the "NEW" version of whatever technology he just purchased can assist you in keeping Tom's focus away from the actual cost of attempting to handle so many tasks at the same time.

Yes, that means you are Rail #4. Though each of your predecessors took a few strides forward, in the end, every one of them failed. You should not even know of their existence. I have sold this information to you as a sign I am here to help you. We will discuss your continual payment at a later time.

All that being said, you know as well as I do that neither the average male nor female can be genuinely successful nor effective in doing more than one thing at a time. So busy-ness can be a disgustingly useful tool.

I continue to watch. Do not disappoint me.

evalS_rekaM :-{(

—

The apostles then rendezvoused with Jesus and reported on all that they had done and taught. Jesus said, "Come off by your-selves; let's take a break and get a little rest." For there was con-stant coming and going. They didn't even have time to eat.

So they got in the boat and went off to a remote place by themselves . . .

MARK 6:30–32

Email 3

FROM: evalS_rekaM@loweryet.net
TO: Rail@hellnet.com
Subject: A Multitude Of Temptation Flops
Received: 01.18.06

Rail,

Very well, I will elaborate re: Rail #'s 1–3. I will not do so because you deserve it or have earned this explanation in any way, but in the hope that by your hearing firsthand what they did and how they failed, your evil will have more depth and be more repugnant than it is at the present time. Further, let me warn you that once you have received this email, if your nightly reports bewailing those preceding you do not cease, saying you will have hell to pay is entirely insufficient. So listen now and learn.

Rail #1, whose abilities to exaggerate, cheat, steal and lie found him lowered in rank far enough to be used as a tool in Tom's life there on earth. Loathsome as it might seem, he began his assignment by seeking to be Tommy's (as R-1 referred to him) friend. He took Tommy in at an early age by telling him he would always be there for him and that he would always provide everything and anything Tommy thought he needed that day. His failure came when the boy's grandfather died from an unexpected heart attack. While R-1 could have used it as an opportunity to lie re: how G_d (do not dare write that name in full!) did not help Tommy, he did not act quickly enough and Tommy then began to wonder whether R-1 could help him in any way . . . and if he could, why didn't he? R-1 was removed from the case.

Rail #2 first let Tom-boy (his own disgusting pet name) get to know him during the teen years, which are such a time of confusion for humans. Strategically, he chose to relentlessly replay Tom-boy's first moment of success in sports. As he grew physically larger and more coordinated than his peers, Tom-boy had become the quarterback of the football team at his high school. In the final home game, Tom-boy threw a wobbly pass, which was carried by the wind just far enough, that his teammate, Samuel Obadiah, was able to catch the ball and then stumble 47 yards for the game's winning touchdown.

Yet because of his own sluggishness, R-2 failed miserably to use this event to cement their relationship. Further, he botched the chance to remind Tom-boy of their growing relationship. R-2 did not use this event as an opportunity to point out to Tom-boy that even if the fickle fans would boo, R-2 would always be there for him.

It was equally unfortunate that the cheerleader, C. J., began to pay attention to Tom-boy and take him to enemy meetings on Sunday. Needless to say, R-2 was immediately removed and to this day prepares billions of mindless multi-mailings focused on broad-chance temptations to all new residents as well as the good news email to millions that they have just won a huge international lottery.

Rail #3 failed when, five years later, he was unable to prevent or break down the marriage between C. J. and Tom. With the birth of their first child, R-3 was yanked from the scene when they had the child baptized, without their believing that the water was truly magic.

You have been trained for and sent to Tom to lure him today. Perhaps the most useful tool attempted by any of your forerunners was that of keeping him focused on victories of the past. No matter what you try, pay attention to how and why your predecessors failed. Learn from their mistakes and get off my back!

evalS_rekaM :-{(

For the third test, the Devil took him on the peak of a huge mountain. He gestured expansively, pointing out all the earth's kingdoms, how glorious they all were. Then he said, "They're yours—lock, stock, and barrel. Just go down on your knees and worship me, and they're yours."

Jesus' refusal was curt: "Beat it, Satan!" He backed his rebuke with a third quotation from Deuteronomy: "Worship the Lord your God, and only him. Serve him with absolute single-heartedness."

MATTHEW 4:8–10

Email 4

FROM: evalS_rekaM@loweryet.net
TO: Rail@hellnet.com
Subject: **Repetition & Busy-ness as Temptation**
Received: 01.24.06

Rail,

When other tools become less effective, you can still keep Tom in the dark by falling back to the "tried and false." Point out to Tom that, regardless of what he already has or what he wants at that moment, better is always available to him and you are the only one with the key to that which is flawless. Since he is fascinated by electronics, keep him hungry for what is most innovative and therefore obviously better. Pop-ups have proven for some to be an expedient means of such an approach.

If that should fail you, encourage him to regularly reminisce on the computers he has owned in the past. Upgrade his own memory as he looks back on the central processing units of his earliest computer days: the 286®, 386®, 486®, Pentium® and all the rest. Then remind him of just a few of the numerous programs he has encountered in the past decade: Acrobat 6®, Corel 6®, Internet Explorer 6 ®, and my personal favorite Windows ME®.

Once he is on board with you there, remind him of the electronic nature of the laptop he has come to rely upon so heavily. Keep him looking for newer, larger, and faster machines as different and therefore more tailor-made to his needs. Occasionally, do all you can to link him into a site with "free" downloads. The more that becomes a habit for him, remind Tom that the best freebies he has found have come from you, and whether they have or not is actually immaterial.

Pay careful attention to the attachments I have sent which list such downloads from your peers whose assignment is to consistently produce freebies to download from the Internet, which are of the most use to our offices. Let me encourage you to regularly touch base with dormaR to upload to your own files the most up to date developments from our techies prior to pushing Tom toward any of the downloads. This will insure that we have sufficient time to attach the most destructively useful COOKIES possible. Send a message with the initial download that he needs to adjust his primary web settings to allow our COOKIE to assist in his receiving all the benefits and future upgrades of the programming he is receiving at no charge.

We will use such program riders to track Tom's emails, his web surfing, and broaden our mailing lists by downloading his personal address files. There is no telling how much we can learn merely by tracking him with the COOKIE attachments so typically used. As with scores of other things, the more he is exposed to them, the less attention he will give them . . . exactly as desired by our lowest leaders.

The longer you keep him interested in that which is newer and therefore bigger and better (and supposedly more useful), the less his attention will be anywhere else. Unless he is extremely abnormal, those steps will assist you in keeping Tom drifting further away from the enemy simply by maintaining clutter in his time which will keep him focused where we want it, anywhere but on the enemy.

Before you respond to this email and continue to waste my time, I fully understand that this is a simple tool. Do not deceive yourself into thinking Tom will see through it as rapidly as you have been trained to observe. Once he begins thinking of you as a trustworthy and useful source of tools, he is many steps closer to being mine, that is, ours. The strategy has worked for generations of those stupid humans doted on by our enemy.

Please note that every step you take or fail to take is carefully recorded.

evalS_rekaM :-{(

Responses I received:

FROM: Adam@anet.net
That sure struck home with me. Like everyone else, I face victories and defeats. Too often I have thought that having more meant success. It could have been more houses to build or a greater number of victories than losses for the team, but the only thing I really want is to be happy and feel like I've made a difference.

FROM: Ryan@rpie.com
The older I get, the more often I recognize that focusing on myself has no genuine value or hope for fulfillment. I'm so grateful that I'm learning to refocus and get my spotlight off of myself and put it on God instead. He never let's me crash into something He can't handle.

No test or temptation that comes your way is beyond the course of what others have had to face. All you need to remember is that God will never let you down; he'll never let you be pushed past your limit; he'll always be there to help you come through it.

1 CORINTHIANS 10:13

Email 5

FROM: evalS_rekaM@loweryet.net
TO: Rail@hellnet.com
Subject: E-mailing a Grudge
Received: 02.06.06

Rail,

We greatly enjoyed your report regarding the fight Tom had with his brother. While it did not involve physical contact, the battle of words can be far more damaging. Tom has always thought that his big brother Andy, imagined himself to be better than anyone else in his family. Andy's vocabulary is large and he thinks quickly. However, speaking quickly is nothing more than Andy's tool for overcoming all who might disagree with him. Add to that the fact that, as referred to earlier, Tom's IQ is 26 points higher than anyone in his family ever has been and you begin to see why your supervisors relish them disagreeing verbally.

When it comes to carrying a grudge, it is likely that a tool that you will find useful at this point is email. Since they will not see each other's faces as they "speak" to each other electronically in this manner, the potential for ongoing battle between them is sizeable. Our most recent study reveals that for 51 percent of the time, emails are misunderstood. From our perspective, that is delightful because the misunderstandings can lead to hurt feelings, which can lead to anger, that can lead to bitterness, and that can create division among humans, who otherwise could have been amicable at one level or another.

They seem to read between emailed words in a manner, which adds the inflection(s) and emphasis they think are most likely. If Andy and Tom have had misunderstandings in the past, their imagined insights can be used to magnify their own importance and lessen that of the one sending it. If handled wisely on your part, the result can be a battle, which partitions Tom from his brother Andy, for the rest of their lives.

Add to that the suffering, which their hatred for each other can cause for their wives and children and you can see why we revel in it. ANY miscommunication can lead to anger or bitterness and we have demographic data, which appears to reveal the lasting depression, which accompanies it all. For what is depression after all but anger turned inwards?

Continue to nurture this fraternal misunderstanding. The longer you can cause their imagined wounds to fester, the less likely it will be for them to get back together and actually like each other as brothers.

evalS_rekaM :-{(

Responses I received:

FROM: Ryan@rpie.com
It is easy to read motives between the lines that aren't really there.

FROM: Colin@hobo.com
I know exactly what you mean. This week, my supervisor hand-delivered a memo to every person on our floor. If you get a message from another person in the corporation and their meaning is at all unclear, don't guess. Pick up your phone and call.

FROM: Adam@anet.net
It's so much more than just being mad for one day over the play that cost your team the game. Friends of our family stopped speaking because one farmed land the other wanted. Rather than talk about it, they chose to be angry with each other the rest of their lives.

—

. . . Keep us alive with three square meals. Keep us forgiven with you and forgiving others. Keep us safe from the Devil and ourselves—You're in charge! You can do anything you want! You're ablaze in beauty! Yes. Yes. Yes.

"In prayer there is a connection between what God does and what you do. You can't get forgiveness from God, for instance, without also forgiving others . . ."

MATTHEW 6:11–14

Email 6

FROM: evalS_rekaM@loweryet.net
TO: Rail@hellnet.com
Subject: Computer Crash=Life Crash
Received: 02.13.06

Rail,

I knew before you reported that Tom's computer had crashed late last night. The viruses and worms that we sent and you forwarded to him were successful in dodging the protective software that Tom had squandered his savings upon. Once flooded, his Random Access Memory (RAM) became more random than he could ever imagine in the way it gathered any information and then became permanently locked.

As he poured repeatedly through the manuals he had never bothered to study until last night, he had no clue where to look or how to make a bit of sense of the hundreds of fine print and hard copy pages before him. And, with his computer entirely frozen up, he had no access whatsoever to websites that he had been lulled into believing would easily repair any difficulty he ever would face. As it was, they proved entirely unusable to him in his efforts to reboot his system.

If all else fails, he can certainly purchase a new computer. Let this computerized failure continue to act as an illustration for you of one of the ways in which you might attack Tom personally. Keep him away from regular contact with the instruction manual that our opponent so pompously claims to have sent to those who seek to follow him. If Tom does not look into G_d's manual on any regular basis, our research team has indicated to me that the likelihood of his doing so is extremely low except for moments when he has the bizarre expectation of receiving whatever aid he requires, and then, in exclusively the manner and time frame he requests.

In addition to that, having never read it before, Tom will make little sense of words G_d (Do not ever let me catch you using that name in full.) claims to have sent. Humans tend to open it, if at all, as a box of magic band-aids or free generic software repairs.

Therefore, when his personal system crashes and he finds himself in the abyss, if Tom insists upon turning to communication from G_d , then do all possible to turn his attention to the most highly confusing phrases possible. Continue to do all conceivable to lead him to think of his situation as hopeless even though, for reasons still unclear, G_d continues to tell people otherwise.

Never forget that you are totally in the deception and temptation business. Do not deceive yourself into thinking that this is a simple emotional issue that will quickly pass. The enemy will use this situation in Tom's life if we do not. I continue to record all you do 24/7.

evalS_rekaM :-{(

Responses I received:

FROM: Ryan@rpie.com
No wonder God left an instruction manual of sorts in His Word. I know I have told my friends many times how often I have read the entire Bible, when really I only know the highlights of the Gospels. But beyond that, there's so much of the time that I have to go to the front of the book to find out the page number for those tiny books of Daniel or James.

Jesus resumed talking to the people, but now tenderly. "The Father has given me all these things to do and say. This is a unique Father-Son operation, coming out of Father and Son intimacies and knowledge. No one knows the Son the way the Father does, nor the Father the way the Son does. But I'm not keeping it to myself; I'm ready to go over it line by line with anyone willing to listen.

"Are you tired? Worn out? Burned out on religion? Come to

me. Get away with me and you'll recover your life. I'll show you how to take a real rest. Walk with me and work with me—watch how I do it. Learn the unforced rhythms of grace. I won't lay anything heavy or ill-fitting on you. Keep company with me and you'll learn to live freely and lightly."

MATTHEW 11:28–30

Email 7

FROM: evalS_rekaM@loweryet.net
TO: Rail@hellnet.com
Subject: Habitual Crashes
Received: 02.18.06

Rail,

Tom has been pushed, lured, and wooed for an extended period of human time. At this stage, it is quite often useful and effective to abuse the tool he considers his conscience. It may prove equally helpful to lay before Tom the foolishness of even entertaining the possibility of forgiveness for half a century of actions.

Recent studies by our demographics department of a variety of bundles of humans vary greatly in their judgments here, but my opinion is that the term "½ a century of sin" has far heavier impact emotionally on most humans than mentioning "fifty years of sin." That said, feel free to study the issue in depth as time allows and use what seems most effective with Tom. Regardless of the manner you may choose, remind Tom frequently of the extended period in which he has regularly chosen to live outside the "be ye perfect" standard which G_d has set. It could be something along this line (perhaps as an email from a guy claiming to be a long-lost college classmate).

Since he attended the University of Iowa back in the 70s and doesn't remember much of what went on there, let alone who all his "classmates" were, that should work. If you choose not to go that way, claim to be from a class he is currently taking online from the University of Ireland Coast (which, by the way, does not exist. We run its bogus version entirely from the home office.) Printed below is a sample of the chat room conversation you might send.

Hey Tom! From our online discussions in the past few months, it seems clear to me that you have chosen to hang onto the pessimistic side of all philosophies.

My own experience along that line is that traveling that road leads one to get stuck with the consequences of sin and I'm not into that.

I suppose it MIGHT be possible that some creator would let such consequences slide for a ticket a guy got for driving too fast, perhaps even the night he said he had spent in jail for excessive drunkenness, but what about cheating on your wife? What if you were like the fellow in Northern Ireland last month who claimed he had purposely killed people by means of numerous hit-and-run car accidents?

As you pursue this, Rail, it is clear to me that you must ask Tom if any G_d really forgives and forgets, with something along these lines:

I doubt it. So do you. Be honest with yourself for a change. If that's your real philosophy there is no way you can measure up to the standards G_d must have set regarding acceptable behaviors. Here's my question for you. Why even bother anymore?

You get my drift here, Rail. Hopelessness is a wonderfully convenient tool.

rekaM_evalS :-{(

—

Responses I received:

FROM: Ryan@rpie.com
Don't you believe it! Don't buy the idea that there's no hope for you! The important thing overlooked in all of this is that no matter how worthless one is and no matter how great the depths of my sin, forgiveness is still possible. It's his forgiveness and not my actions that made me right with Him It's never anything I do. God is a forgiving God. In thinking about it, I often remember what Jesus told the thief on the cross.

—

When the Philistines got word that David had been made king over all Israel, they came on the hunt for him. David heard of it and went down to the stronghold. When the Philistines arrived, they deployed their forces in Raphaim Valley.

Then David prayed to God: "Shall I go up and fight the Philistines? Will you help me beat them?"

"Go up," God replied. "Count on me. I'll help you beat them."

2 SAMUEL 5:17–20

Email 8

FROM: evalS_rekaM@loweryet.net
TO: Rail@hellnet.com
Subject: Short-sighted vs. Long-sighted
Received: 02.24.06

Rail,

I despise the times families gather to celebrate anything. I could barely tolerate it as your temptee's family sang: "Happy Birthday to You! Happy Birthday to You! Happy Birthday, Dear Tom! Happy Birthday to you!" I never cease to be amazed that human creatures allow themselves to focus on the importance of life only one day per year. Lest I brag wastefully, let me merely convey to you that the initial idea of birthday cake once a year was my own. Regardless of what you have heard, I was still the model for the one below me who filched my scheme. So while others claim credit, celebrating once a year in this manner was MY idea. At any rate, the entire marketing department has executed the plan sublimely and has successfully duped human creatures into believing that being alive is a gift worth celebrating only once a year. Do all you can to keep Tom focused on annual events. Better yet, help him look at decades or lifetimes.

If his concentration remains exclusively on the long haul, Tom is far less likely to see each moment as a step closer to his last. As long as he is looking far ahead, it will be easier to make the here and now seem so insignificant that he really shouldn't bother himself with it. Once you have him looking at the long haul, slap him with the unexpected unfair ending of the lives of others. Remind Tom that his neighbor down the street had his life come to an end unexpectedly. While the man who died was a year older than his wife, he was, to the day, the same age as Tom.

If he should begin looking at daily incidents at all, keep Tom on as many email listings as possible to keep flooding him with what appears to be the most recent viral disorder striking others. If the disease is sickening others, isn't it possible to strike him as well? Add to that the enduring side effects and weaknesses he imagines he has following the surgery he had eight months ago. While it might seem so trivial to even dream that having his tonsils removed could cause him any genuine problem, keep reminding him that his birthday is coming up, and how many others has he ever heard of who had their tonsils out when they were 50?

So, keep him concentrated on what is distant and keep him on the emotional edge by the most insignificant trivia he faces each day. Sublime examples include fresher breath, nicer socks, and fewer hairs left behind in the brush. Best of all, if you can move him that far, remind him often that he is the only one ever to have suffered in exactly this way.

Short-sighted or long-sighted? It makes no difference which is truly worse. Keep shuffling what he sees and hears so that his focus tomorrow is not the same as yesterday or today. Keep shuffling and keep him confused.

evalS_rekaM :-{(

Responses I received:

FROM: Kim@anet.net
When our little girl had tubes put in her ear this week, I came face to face with every single day mattering. I thought again about how much can be done medically for us here.

FROM : Cory@hobo.com
Her cousin, our oldest boy, had the same thing last month. What surprised me was that God would give gifts to people to help others like that. Wow.

FROM: Katie@rpie.com
Regardless of how many years we have been here, each moment of every day is a gift from the Lord. It is so easy to look beyond today without thanking Him for today as we are praying through our list of what we would really like tomorrow.

—

Jesus knew exactly what they were thinking and said, "Why all this gossipy whispering? Which is simpler: to say 'I forgive your sins,' or to say 'Get up and start walking'? Well, just so it's clear that I'm the Son of Man and authorized to do either, or both . . ." He now spoke directly to the paraplegic: "Get up. Take your bedroll and go home." Without a moment's hesitation, he did it—got up, took his blanket, and left for home, giving glory to God all the way. The people rubbed their eyes, incredulous—and then also gave glory to God. Awestruck, they said, "We've never seen anything like that!"

LUKE 5:22–26

Email 9

FROM: evalS_rekaM@loweryet.net
TO: Rail@hellnet.com
Subject: Sick and tired of being sick and tired
Received: 03.06.06

Rail,

The discovery of Tom's seizure disorder is really not a discovery at all. It is merely an admission of reality on Tom's part. He has suffered from seizures of numerous types off and on for over half of his life, yet being well aware of the societal luggage and the closing of doors epilepsy would carry with it, the dozen physicians he has seen regarding this illness have built in alternative names that would not carry as much baggage.

My personal favorite is that of labeling his symptoms as a complex-partial seizure disorder. It can be charmingly deceptive as a medical title and is in fact the name your predecessor wooed Tom into using for over thirteen years as a tool for lying to others, deceiving himself, and most importantly, seeking to conceal his shame for not being a person independent or strong enough to cope with anything that should come his way.

We have discussed on numerous occasions already that, at least by the standards humans so foolishly cling to, in order to proclaim his value, Tom lets it be known that he is an exceptionally intelligent man. Yet as his illness has progressed, he has watched himself slip further away from being able to keep his illness hidden as both the severity and frequency of seizures have increased.

As stated before, the very title "medicine" is delightfully deceptive as it carries with it the hope of instant or at least substantial cure. Yet for these many years, medicines have not provided Tom with the cure for which he has longed. Whether it be Dilantin ®, Tegretol ®, Lamictal ®, Felbatol ® or half a dozen more drugs, each drug has proven itself to be useless in his case. As each has failed, fear and gloominess have become larger parts of his life. As he has repeatedly tumbled between fear, anxiety, anger and shame, you have successfully used depression to encourage Tom to swallow his anger and fear for yet one more day rather than express them and let all those around him know he carries a shameful disease.

Tom survived the surgery in which they removed the portion of his brain which technically caused the disorder and we grieve that he did not become a mere vegetable. Nonetheless, continue to remind Tom that the surgery took place six months ago and physicians are still searching for medicines which will bestow upon him a genuine cure. After all, shouldn't the surgery remove his need for medicine? What was the point of such trauma if he needs to swallow (and pay for) more pills today than he did then? Add to that an endless string of reminders that Tom's neurologist is himself dying of brain cancer. As he dwells once again on that news, the fragment of hope to which Tom clings will be shaken once more.

As always, through this all, keep Tom focused upon himself alone. Never let him even consider the countless others who are plagued with the identical system failure or numerous others. If he should stumble in that general direction, point out the lie that that even if others are sick, they are not as afflicted with illness as he is and there is nothing worse than what he has had to deal with. If you succeed in keeping his focus so fully on himself and his illness, then the odds of his calling out to G_d for help remain slim.

Keep up the miserable work!

rekaM_evalS :-{(

From the Chat Room:

FROM: Lilly@firstborn.edu
This made me stop to think how many times I have been more concerned with my own needs than with those of others.

FROM: Thatch@akson.org

I found myself thinking out loud with my wife, asking her how many times I have been so focused on what I do and who I am that I have missed out on seeing the needs of others around me.

FROM: Jack@west1.net

It struck me that every one of us has some event or illness or weakness in our lives that will, if we let it, keep us totally focused on ourselves and no one else. But if we will look beyond the mirror, God can do incredible things with us.

If I had a mind to brag a little, I could probably do it without looking ridiculous, and I'd still be speaking plain truth all the way. But I'll spare you. I don't want anyone imagining me as anything other than the fool you'd encounter if you saw me on the street or heard me talk.

Because of the extravagance of those revelations, and so I wouldn't get a big head, I was given the gift of a handicap to keep me in constant touch with my limitations. Satan's angel did his best to get me down; what he in fact did was push me to my knees. No danger then of walking around high and mighty! At first I didn't think of it as a gift, and begged God to remove it. Three times I did that, and then he told me,

My grace is enough; it's all you need.

My strength comes into its own in your weakness.

Once I heard that, I was glad to let it happen. I quit focusing on the handicap and began appreciating the gift. It was a case of Christ's strength moving in on my weakness. Now I take limitations in stride, and with good cheer, these limitations that cut me down to size—abuse, accidents, opposition, bad breaks. I just let Christ take over! And so the weaker I get, the stronger I become.

2 CORINTHIANS 12:6–10

Email 10

FROM: evalS_rekaM@loweryet.net
TO: Rail@hellnet.com
Subject: **Using Tom's Work Against Him**
Received: 03.13.06

Feeble-Minded Rail:

It is plain to see that Tom is a workaholic. Why is it that you even wonder or doubt it at all? It is not as simple as your idiotic equation which claims that all who labor over 50 hours a week are susceptible to workaholism while those with part time jobs are not. There is no magic number of hours labored which determines if Tom works too much.

I know the query you are composing to send, so let me clarify your mind for just a moment. It boils down to this: If Tom finds his sole sense of value and accomplishment in what he does at work, he is a workaholic.

The obvious application of this principle for your use is this—find as many means as possible to cause Tom to feel worthwhile at work and do all possible to steer him away from anything or anyone away from the office. Then as he senses labor being the genuine meaning of his life, begin to call down to looF rekaM whose assignment is Jacob S., Tom's boss. looF rekaM has acquired a special adeptness at persuading Jacob to consistently seek the short-comings (either real or imagined) of employees. With Tom's perspective that doing more leads to human value, looF rekaM can assist you with leaving Tom more desolate every time his boss points out all that Tom has done which does not measure up.

Living as a workaholic, hoping for lasting impact and change, can be most useful with those who doubt their ability to do anything else and with those who fear the changes required when anything changes. Keep Tom wed to the standards of success that anyone other than he himself sets. Each time you are able to do so, keep Tom clinging to the lie that the single lasting value he ever will obtain can only be generated at work. Do that and you keep him in the dimness we desire.

Your success makes my mouth water at the prospect of bringing Tom into the darkness forever. Until that happens, I record every moment of what you do 24/7.

evalS_rekaM :-{((

—

Responses I received:

FROM: Colin@hobo.com
When I read this, I found myself wondering why so much of our culture is focused on producing more of what we can see in order to make a difference, as if the only thing that matters is what we can see. I have a large number of friends who work for Fortune 500 corporations, and so much of the time they act as if every breath comes from the ones who sign their paycheck.

FROM: Adam@anet.net
I work for myself, but the same thing is true about me when it comes to where my focus is when I work. Our culture offers programs to help people get away from being addicted to booze and drugs and gambling, but not to working too much. It's almost an insider's joke to get together with my friends, sigh a little, and then say, "Yeah, I know, I'm a workaholic. But if that's the worst problem I have, I've got it made." What a lie.

FROM: Ryan@rpie.com
True. It sounds a great deal like only bigger being better. Somehow we mold ourselves around the idea that the only definition of success that is valid has to be measured by the words "substantial, " "profitable," "extensive, " or at least "developing."

—

As they continued their travel, Jesus entered a village. A woman by the name of Martha welcomed him and made him feel quite at home. She had a sister, Mary, who sat before the Master, hanging on every word he said. But Martha was pulled away by all she had to do in the kitchen. Later, she stepped in, interrupting them. "Master, don't you care that my sister has abandoned the kitchen to me? Tell her to lend me a hand."

The Master said, "Martha, dear Martha, you're fussing far too much and getting yourself worked up over nothing. One thing only is essential, and Mary has chosen it—it's the main course, and won't be taken from her."

LUKE 10:38–42

Email 11

FROM: evalS_rekaM@loweryet.net
TO: Rail@hellnet.com
Subject: Firewalls
Received: 03.18.06

Rail:

I loathe to tell you this, but your attempt to slip past the edge of the firewalls has been utterly disgusting and those in the offices further down and further out have screamed their approval throughout this past week. It was one thing to get Tom stuck in pondering his own frailty, but attacking him ceaselessly in the death of his friend Jake, is a cruel tasteless manner of slapping Tom when he already hurts. Every time I described it, the cheers began all over again.

I ordered you earlier to stay out of this chat room. It is reserved only for those with ranks far lower than yours. However since you are here, I will answer your question. The effectiveness of your methods was simple. Listen carefully. Beyond losing a friend, Tom's emotional edge was saddened in the many ways he felt he had failed Jake, remembering how long it had been since he had spoken with Jake, and the days he had let Jake down by lying to him, saying that he was sick and could not go on a double date when the reality was that he snuck out later that night with C. J., that wretched cheerleader he eventually married.

It grieves me to repeat it, but you have done so well in using guilt to bring deep pain into Tom's life that rumors here continue re: Natas himself considering demoting you. Nonetheless, do not let that change your focus. The firewall's design is to capture ideas that have broken through. To keep things off balance as long as possible, let me suggest a rotation between three tools that others have used with great success in similar situations:

1. Self-Centeredness—Help and encourage Tom to focus repeatedly on what HE has lost, his own pain, his own regrets over what he failed to do with or for his best friend.

2. Anger—Point out every day how unjust it is for Jake to die when _____ lives. Fill in the blank with the name of a criminal from the recent news or an individual Tom already hates. Be sure to remind Tom that it is unfair for the family to live with such heartache after Jake has already passed on. Of course we recognize the foolishness of that non-reason, but he won't for some time. The longer you can keep Tom angry, the better.

3. Depression—When efforts to keep him angry begin to prove ineffective, help Tom turn the anger inside. Often the simple change in word from anger to depression works wonders. Our staffs there have done wonders to make anger acceptable and depression shameful in their age and culture. For one, he can be imprisoned, while for the other, he will be medicated. Given Tom's personality profile, it is highly likely his history of depression is something he would want as few as possible to know about.

Given the nature of the culture, products have been developed to minimize pain. If he succumbs to that avenue, remind him daily of the shame he must bear in not being strong enough to get through this on his own. The enemy will not permit Tom to stay there nearly as long as you think. Make the most of it.

evalS_rekaM :-{(

Responses I received:

FROM: Colin@hobo.com
Doesn't it surprise you that sometimes, just when everything seems to be going great, that's when it seems like one more problem blows up in your face? Isn't there any end to the garbage that comes my way?

FROM: Adam@anet.net
I know what you mean. Last week our car's engine blew out. The week before that, I fell at work and broke my wrist. The week before that, our water heater went out. Nothing bad happened for a month, and then it was like there was no end to it.

—

"I pulled you in from all over the world, called you in from every dark corner of the earth, Telling you, 'You're my servant, serving on my side. I've picked you. I haven't dropped you.' Don't panic. I'm with you. There's no need to fear for I'm your God. I'll give you strength. I'll help you. I'll hold you steady, keep a firm grip on you.

"Count on it: Everyone who had it in for you will end up out in the cold—real losers. Those who worked against you will end up empty-handed—nothing to show for their lives . . ."

ISAIAH 41:9–11

Email 12

FROM: evalS_rekaM@loweryet.net
TO: Rail@hellnet.com
Subject: Keep Him Away From Church
Received: 03.24.06

Rail,

I know his despicable wife, C. J., has convinced Tom to consider returning to that weekly event on his only day off. Your question regarding his temptation to walk away from the darkness was well-timed and proves that you have paid more attention to him than I believed.

There are several ways to approach him at this point. The simplest and most straight-forward is to agree with him regarding the importance of this choice. Remind Tom of the many balls he has in the air and how he needs to discern their individual value within the greater scheme of life.

Given the tone of some of the church-club products he has seen advertised so often, it should be simple to get him to take a retreat to contemplate this choice. While nataS generally despises such events, in this case it could be a helpful tool. The retreat event is not taking place for two months. That will give you 60 days to woo Tom away and to distract him.

Further, the topic of the retreat is being sold as what one should do in order to work more effectively for the enemy. That makes your task simpler. After all, Tom has never truly served the enemy, so having him be confronted and challenged to live as the weak-minded, weak-willed slave of G_d every moment of Tom's life will be a very large step, far greater than the simple choice his spouse suggests of going to the weekly meetings with her.

All that being said, the argument Tom had with his wife last night could prove helpful as well. C. J.'s primary argument was that they need to work together to raise their children and that Tom is serving as a poor example by not attending the weekly events with her. As he contemplates that, suggest to him the importance of teaching their children to choose. After all, isn't he teaching that very thing by choosing not to attend weekend events?

Based upon reports from those specializing in children in that part of the world, we have come to understand that those in Tom's shoes have, through their example of self-centeredness and spiritual laziness, communicated to their sons and daughters that they need not ever darken the door of such a place. That is, after all, what they have observed in their fathers.

So keep Tom telling C. J. that he is considering change, and keep him sleeping whenever she darkens the door of enemy headquarters.

evalS_rekaM :-{(

Responses I received:

FROM: Adam@anet.net
I shudder every time I imagine what God must think on a day when we don't worship because we're too busy.

FROM: Katie@rpie.com
That makes me think of what God must think about the excuses I use on a day that I make no time to be alone with Him. You know what I mean, a day when you're so busy that you don't talk to Him or even nod your head towards Him by reading a little bit of His Word.

FROM: Cory@hobo.com
Can you imagine what it might look like on stage? The lead actress is crying out to the Lord, but God keeps falling asleep every time she tries to talk to Him. I'm grateful that's not ever the case.

If you decide that it's a bad thing to worship God, then choose a god you'd rather serve—and do it today. Choose one of the gods your ancestors worshiped from the country beyond The River, or one of the gods of the Amorites, on whose land you're now living. ". . . As for me and my family, we'll worship God."

JOSHUA 24:15

Email 13

FROM: evalS_rekaM@loweryet.net
TO: Rail@hellnet.com
Subject: Tuning us In
Received: 03.30.06

Rail,

Your apparent impact upon C. J. has caused me to reconsider the wisdom of our previous generational focus on one human at a time. After I forwarded your pleading request, you have been granted short-term permission from those below me to pursue mass marketing the concept of selfishness as you described it.

Ego stroking has been used in exploiting humans for generations as a means of successfully turning their attention upon themselves. As you reported regarding the lifestyle that C. J. has pursued, I was not surprised that she is regularly involved with worshipping our enemy. It was a pleasant surprise however to learn that she is so open to judging others as less spiritual and therefore less worthy than herself.

If her judgmental nature is indeed the avenue you intend to pursue in reaching C. J. and others like her, let me recommend that you include the following steps:

First, define holy. How you define it for him has no importance whatsoever except to say that your definition must be different than that which G_d has passed on. If you change the definition to suit the time of year it is, so much the better. Regardless of how you define it for her today, let it be a bit different every day.

Second, use a variety of informational sources. Recent rumors of her area have shown that many people read newspapers; some at least briefly watch news on television; and many others browse the Internet. However, the source, which surprised many in my department, was the number whose primary source of information was the radio.

Finally, do not allow yourself to be lulled into believing that old-fashioned means something is useless. Since C. J. travels a great deal for her work, she is likely to listen to communication on the old-fashioned radio broadcasting system. Especially during late night hours, your opportunities to reach those who are an audience trapped within their vehicles increases and weariness on the side of the listener makes it simpler to slip a diversity of ideas into the market without its real danger being noticed.

If the number of things claiming to be true is increased, it is possible that even a religious person like C. J. may be lulled into the point of asking whether or not a number of ideas may be equally true. If that is the case, how can she make any claim that her ideology is one bit more valid than that of any other human?

Report regularly to me regarding the impact these steps have upon C. J. and then second-handedly upon Tom as you market these ideas to her and as Tom is regularly exposed to her.

rekaM_evalS :-{(

From the Chat Room:

FROM: Harry@humboldt.com
I do find that I have to listen carefully when I am driving home. After a hard day in the office, I tend to just veg out and not really pay much attention to what's on.

FROM: Jack@west1.net
I have had the same thing so many times that I have started carrying CD's in the car of things I know I can believe, rather than get sucked into a lie without realizing it.

—

"Confront me with the truth and I'll shut up, show me where I've gone off the track. Honest words never hurt anyone . . ."

JOB 6:24–25

Email 14

FROM: evalS_rekaM@loweryet.net
TO: Rail@hellnet.com
Subject: Fear
Received: 04.06.06

Rail,

Fear is a splendid implement. Regular mention in the news of the most recent crash, catastrophe, worm or virus can plant seeds, water them, encourage their growth, and effectively freeze Tom where he is at this moment. Your report regarding Tom's childhood memory as Tommy regarding the day "Stevie" the school bully beat him up can be especially useful here. Remind him of how it felt to be backed up against the lockers in the hallway of the middle school.

Once you have him mentally standing there, help him jump back to the weeks prior to the first punch when Stevie singled him out on the school bus, called him names he would not repeat to anyone even today, and threatened Tommy repeatedly with the beating he would be getting as soon as he could get Tommy all by himself.

The belief that one is isolated whenever something formidable is faced is a splendid fuel for fear. The oppositions Tom faces today are different from that fight in the hallway as a kid, but his terror can be identical and the terror can lead to panic to the point where Tom freezes when he faces difficult choices. Once Tom is frozen, unable to choose how to face today's challenge, then strike him with the recollection of that fight in the hallway.

You will need to cloud his memories just a bit because Tommy just received one blow in the face that day. Then he chose to stand there to face the bully, no matter what came next. Then the whole thing ended when the principal of the school ran down the hall, screaming their names and telling them to break it up and move on. On the school bus the next morning Stevie sat down behind Tommy, leaned forward, and the last sentence ever spoken between them was that he could not believe that Tommy was so much tougher than he had ever guessed.

Help Tom remember the beating and the feeling of dread he felt as the showdown approached. Keep him focused there and fear will continue to be a useful tool. Let him remember facing the worst and moving on and you will have wasted a great deal. Tom will be reminded that it made a difference when he stepped out and took a stand even when he was afraid. Do not, I repeat, DO NOT let Tom drift that way or fear is no longer a useful tool.

Know that I am required to file daily reports on each of you. I will certainly note your success or failure in how you encourage fear or how you fail. 24/7.

evalS_rekaM :-{(

Responses I received:

FROM: Katie@rpie.com
Ryan forwarded the last email to me. He said he was so sure it talked about me, but the minute I got done reading it, I couldn't help but laugh.

FROM: Ryan@rpie.com
When I finally got her to tell me why she thought it was funny, she just said that the first person she thought of when she read it was me. When I thought about what she said, I realized we were both right. Fear is miserable. We both are afraid, just afraid of different things.

". . . Haven't I commanded you? Strength! Courage! Don't be timid; don't get discouraged. God, your God, is with you every step you take."

JOSHUA 1:9

Email 15

FROM: evalS_rekaM@loweryet.net
TO: Rail@hellnet.com
Subject: The Use Of The Polka
Received: 04.13.06

Rail,

Let me point out something you seem to have missed when you downloaded the email Tom sent to his mother about the dance class his son Zach, is taking in college. As I scan the messages you sent, Zach told his father that the polka was one of the dances he hoped to learn well in the weeks to come. If your knowledge of Tom's generation was at all detailed, you should have noted that they hated their parents (at least for awhile) but for reasons unknown, loved and respected their grandparents. In my momentary glimpse at the info regarding Tom's grandparents, Frank and Lillian, they taught Tom to polka when he was young. Forty years later, Zach treats it as new, creative, and desirable.

Remember how often I have told you to keep changing the ways used to tempt Tom? [See emails dated 06-06-03, 06-13-04 and 06-06-05 to name a few occurrences off the top of my head.] The point is that temptation does not mean developing something never tried before. To satisfy your mathematical inclination, illogical as it may seem: **CHANGE IN TEMPTATION ≠ NEW TEMPTATION.** An enticement is not new merely because its outward show is different. The tried and false are so often the most easily effective tools. Look back for a moment at the means used on Frank and Lillian, dressing them a bit differently, tweaking them so they sound contemporary and you will have done nothing more than present the same old temptation all over again. Do not be more of a fool than you have shown yourself to be. Your assignment is not to create new. It is plainly to drag down all in Tom's life that could possibly impact or move him toward any affirmative conduct, demeanor or behavior. Every time you catch yourself doing anything else, remember the polka and go back once again to using whatever has already been used in Tom's past most effectively.

So get back to the past.

I continue to monitor your every move, future, present, and past.

evalS_rekaM :-{(

From the Chat Room:

FROM: Lilly@firstborn.edu
I remember what my grandpa told me about how much his dad learned in the few weeks grandpa had been off for his basic training for armed forces. He was so sure his father was an idiot until he left home for a little while and then realized that his dad had not been so dumb after all. That sounds like exactly the way I thought of my dad too. Only after I was away from home for a while, did I realize the same thing grandpa did about his dad. I guess Satan doesn't really change his way of attacking us very much at all does he?

FROM: Jack@west1.net
You're right. Every one of us is tempted more than once. We shouldn't be surprised that it happens over and over in the same areas of our lives. But God has ALWAYS been bigger than the troubles I've faced.

When he came back to his disciples, he found them sound asleep. He said to Peter, "Can't you stick it out with me a single hour? Stay alert; be in prayer so you don't wander into temptation without even knowing you're in danger. There is a part of you that is eager, ready for anything in God. But there's another part that's as lazy as an old dog sleeping by the fire."

MATTHEW 26:40–41

Email 16

FROM: evalS_rekaM@loweryet.net
TO: Rail@hellnet.com
Subject: Blame-shifting
Received: 04.18.0

Rail,

As Tom and C. J. continue to struggle with the differences between them, you are the fool of all fools if you fail to take advantage of it. Of course C. J. is right when she concludes Tom spends an unhealthy amount of time at work. She has seen through the lie of the job falling apart without one person. With C. J. late getting home last night, use that hour as his excuse for her holding him to a standard she never keeps herself. Point out to Tom that if working too much is a problem, then C. J. is clearly the one who needs counseling, not him.

Then point to and do all you can to inflate the value of where Tom has invested his life. Remind him of the benefits he is sure so many others have received due to his labors. We both know that the new computer friendly software will never work at all with the most recent random memory access/roam developments. However, that makes no difference whatsoever. Tom has been convinced that his work will give him lasting meaning. Keep his focus there and away from this truly life-warping ideology C. J. has swallowed.

Whenever Tom is chastised or belittled for doing one thing wrong, remind him of three places others close to him have failed, especially if their action is related to what he did in even the most remote way. Then it must, of course, be the other person's fault and not his own.

Rail, can you imagine how few would end up stepping further in and down if they genuinely believed and lived as if any of their value came from something other than what they want to do? Ugh! The very thought makes me shudder.

evalS_rekaM :-{(

Responses I received:

—

FROM: Kim@anet.net
It's easy for me to recognize where those around me have placed their values. It makes me wonder what others see in me.

—

God saw what they had done, that they had turned away from their evil lives. He did change his mind about them. What he said he would do to them he didn't do . . .

Jonah was furious. He lost his temper . . .

He went out of the city to the east and sat down in a sulk. He put together a makeshift shelter of leafy branches and sat there in the shade to see what would happen to the city. God arranged for a broad-leafed tree to spring up. It grew over Jonah to cool him off and get him out of his angry sulk. Jonah was pleased and enjoyed the shade. Life was looking up.

But then God sent a worm. By dawn of the next day, the worm had bored into the shade tree and it withered away. The sun came up and God sent a hot, blistering wind from the east. The sun beat down on Jonah's head and he started to faint. He prayed to die: "I'm better off dead!"

Then God said to Jonah, "What right do you have to get angry about this shade tree?" Jonah said, "Plenty of right. It's made me angry enough to die!"

God said, "What's this? How is it that you can change your feelings from pleasure to anger overnight about a mere shade tree that you did nothing to get? You neither planted nor watered it. It grew up one night and died the next night. So, why can't I likewise change what I feel about Nineveh from anger to pleasure, this big city of more than a hundred and twenty thousand childlike people who don't yet know right from wrong, to say nothing of all the innocent animals?"

JONAH 3:10, 4:1, 5–10

Email 17

FROM: evalS_rekaM@loweryet.net
TO: Rail@hellnet.com
Subject: Trojan Horse
Received: 04.24.06

Rail,

The Trojan horse could provide what you have been so unable to touch otherwise. Once used by an army in the ancient past, this simple toy is an analogy, for hiding the genuine content of lies in something that looks large and enjoyable can prove delightfully deadly. Before I go further, you need to know that your situation has been discussed at a lower level, handed back up to me, and I in turn pass it up to you. Let it suffice to say that failure in this area will be most unpleasant for you.

It is acknowledged that you are indeed in dire straits due to the talker who snatched Tom's attentiveness last week. Yet the orders you receive are to develop and execute all possible techniques to encourage Tom to conjure up his own priceless value before the enemy. Since C. J.'s meeting place was at the station Tom heard the speaker, you need to help his thoughts focus on what he owes the building in which they meet, and not the enemy it stands for but the building itself. Thoughts along these lines may prove useful:

"If I help paint the building, perhaps He will value me more highly."

"If that's not enough, as an architect, I could always donate a design for a new and larger building."

"If even that is inadequate, maybe I could cash in retirement accounts or investments, give them all (or at least part of them) to a building fund.

"Certainly, I will be more of an insider with him than if I were not doing as much, and it is clear that I will be more flawless than anyone else in the club."

If you can steer Tom in that direction, he will spend the rest of his existence there seeking bigger, better, more secure (and more visible) manners in which he can earn the enemy's favor. It continues to confound those further down than me, but that strategy is not something the enemy ever seems to find useful. Instead, he continues to simply accept those who call out to him. So keep Tom focusing on events where his participation can earn his way into the enemy's favor. Then you will have a hope and he will not.

I caution you again, do not let him see the hopelessness of seeking to deserve the enemy's friendship. Keep him focused on being better than others by buying his way in.

Those down below are recording every move you make.

evalS_rekaM :-{(

Responses I received:

FROM: Adam@anet.net
The guys on my softball team and I were talking over pizza last night when we started reliving the greatest plays we had ever made. I asked my best friend if I would still have been as good for the team if I hadn't hit that 9th inning home run. He laughed, poked me and said, "Sure you will, but not quite as good." When I got a copy of this email, it made me wonder what things I was doing in order to get God to like me more.

FROM: Ryan@rpie.com
Yeah. As if we could do anything. If we could do anything to earn our way into heaven, why would we need Jesus?

FROM: Colin@hobo.com
Why would God have let His Son go through all that on the cross if we could somehow do it on our own?

Now God has us where he wants us, with all the time in this world and the next to shower grace and kindness upon us in Christ Jesus. Saving is all his idea, and all his work. All we do is trust him enough to let him do it. It's God's gift from start to finish! We don't play the major role. If we did, we'd probably go around bragging that we'd done the whole thing! No, we neither make nor save ourselves. God does both the making and saving. He creates each of us by Christ Jesus to join him in the work he does, the good work he has gotten ready for us to do, work we had better be doing.

EPHESIANS 2:7–10

Email 18

FROM: evalS_rekaM@loweryet.net
TO: Rail@hellnet.com
Subject: Meaningless Road Signs
Received: 04.30.06

Rail,

After consulting with my lower superiors we agree that your evaluation of Tom's most recent speeding ticket can be a productive opportunity for your input into his life. A preliminary web search regarding speeding tickets indicates over a million tickets were dispensed by those pretending to enforce laws in his part of the nation recently. While less than 2 percent of co-offenders have opposed their tickets, we have agreed that having Tom fight his ticket in court will be a tremendous idea on various grounds.

First of all, Tom is genuinely guilty. He was driving at sixty-six miles per hour in a geographical region of his hometown that was clearly marked by six signs as a 25 miles per hour zone. Remind him repeatedly that in the recent past over 60 million tickets of this nature were bestowed upon others in his country. It is commonly argued that the places where such tickets are written are little more than traps.

While we do enjoy snaring people in their sin, we have found that getting them to deny their sin can be far more useful for us. If you are able to have Tom repeat the lie regarding his innocence frequently, it is likely that he will begin to believe it himself.

If you will check the story out completely at http://articles.moneycentral.msn.com, you will see that a few years ago an attorney of New York encouraged humans to cling to a "stay in the pack" mentality when it came to the speed of their vehicle. As we later discussed it among ourselves, we determined that we might be able to use the pack mentality to steer humans in many directions and the plans for this are currently assigned to the demonic tools development department and will be forwarded to you once they have been completed.

In addition to the limits placed on their speed, I point you toward a few of the other restrictions humans have placed upon each other which we have found to be valuable in feeding their rebellion against authority. NO PASSING is my personal favorite. I learned yesterday of another serious accident caused by a young man refusing to believe that the zone for not passing applied to him.

While it does seem more effective with the young, it also has proven useful with males when their tempters have encouraged them to show their masculinity by beating out the potential accident by passing others in areas where it is impossible for them to see if other vehicles approach them. Signs that demand that humans STOP or YIELD have proven themselves advantageous to us for similar reasons.

The entire point of this temptation is not to prove that Tom is right, nor is it to prove that the law is not. Our statistics show that if you will use it as a means of him exhibiting his superiority or his manhood it can be a very useful tool indeed.

Continue to report the results of this incident to us so that we can add it to our database in the development department and make it available to your peers.

Monitoring your movements and temptation tools used has increased in intensity so do not allow yourself to slip into the comfort zone.

rekaM_evalS :-{(

From the Chat Room:

FROM: Jack@west1.net
I've often wondered why the people who pass me on the interstate seem to think the law applies to everybody but them.

FROM: Thatch@akson.org
What it makes me wonder is where else I have developed that habit.

—

. . . If death got the upper hand through one man's wrongdoing, can you imagine the breathtaking recovery life makes, sovereign life, in those who grasp with both hands this wildly extravagant life-gift, this grand setting-everything-right, that the one man Jesus Christ provides?

Here it is in a nutshell: Just as one person did it wrong and got us in all this trouble with sin and death, another person did it right and got us out of it. But more than just getting us out of trouble, he got us into life! One man said no to God and put many people in the wrong; one man said yes to God and put many in the right.

All that passing laws against sin did was produce more law-breakers. But sin didn't, and doesn't, have a chance in competition with the aggressive forgiveness we call grace. When it's sin versus grace, grace wins hands down. All sin can do is threaten us with death, and that's the end of it. Grace, because God is putting everything together again through the Messiah, invites us into life—a life that goes on and on and on, world without end.

Romans 5:17–21

Email 19

FROM: evalS_rekaM@loweryet.net
TO: Rail@hellnet.com
Subject: Pre-Modern, Modern, Post-Modern Or What?
Received: 05.06.06

Rail,

I, too, receive information that regularly contemplates and evaluates the potential impacts of mutations of human communication. Yes, I have heard of blackberry thumb messaging, media multi-tasking, cell phones of all descriptions, DVDs, MP3s and numerous formats for text messaging. While his kids are often simply referred to as Generation M (Media), your comments regarding Tom and his post-modern perspective on life affirm once again your need for continuous training.

We continue to plant a variety of philosophical images in contemporary films. Let them be a helpful tool as you seek to direct Tom's focus. If handled properly, you can bring Tom to the point of trusting that his options will be infinite when he dies. Reinforce this idea that Tom can only achieve such a wonder if he is sincere about what he thinks he believes.

Once you have him at this point, proceed with caution, for Tom will be at grave crossroads. If he adopts the ideology of all things being right and equally useful, acceptable and/or correct, you can begin to reel him in. If he ponders the possibility of only one choice per situation in what the enemy refers to as right, true, or holy, move quickly. If he adopts that focus, Tom will be so much further into the light that simple tools will be of less use for you in the future when it comes to your deceiving him.

To keep him away from the crossroads, make hefty use of vintage colloquialisms such as "Try and try again." Then as Tom repeatedly falls short of perfection, what is there that says he will not be able in the future to evaluate the results, rewind the clock, and choose again? You may find value in developing the relationship with the new husband of his wife's maid of honor, Frank.

At a wedding last week, Frank was telling the holier-than-thou man performing the wedding that he firmly believed the enemy would have many standing outside the gate looking longingly into heaven at the end of human time. Then, realizing how sincere all these people had been, the enemy himself would withdraw the ridiculous standard of a life without sin or trusting his son to pay for their sin, realize what great people they really were and say, "Oh guys, come on in!"

Pre-modern, modern, or post-modern? It really makes no difference. As long as you keep Tom focused on the thought that many choices lead to the same result, it could not matter less what term he uses to describe it. Be quick to listen to Tom as he ponders. Be even quicker to reply.

evalS_rekaM :-{(

Responses I received:

FROM: Ryan@rpie.com
I've heard the same level of thought so many times. You know, that God is really a good old boy who lets all the other good old boys in.

FROM: Colin@hobo.com
You're so right. If it wasn't for God's grace, none of us would be with Him. With that in mind, how can we ever focus on anyone else?

Do you see what this means—all these pioneers who blazed the way, all these veterans cheering us on? It means we'd better get on with it. Strip down, start running—and never quit! No extra spiritual fat, no parasitic sins. Keep your eyes on Jesus, who both began and finished this race we're in. Study how he did it. Because he never lost sight of where he was headed—that exhilarating finish in and with God—he could put up with anything along the way: cross, shame, whatever. And now he's there, in the place of honor, right alongside God . . .

HEBREWS 12:1–2

Email 20

FROM: evalS_rekaM@loweryet.net
TO: Rail@hellnet.com
Subject: Free Vacation!
Received: 05.13.06

Rail,

Tom's promotion at work can be an excellent opportunity! The spiritual luggage that often accompanies such recognition often simplifies our use of such tiny things to highlight their self-focus. Let me encourage you here to log into your intern's promotional database of free vacations. Let Tom know that if he will only give us the tiniest bit of time, he will then receive meals, relaxation, travel and a soft sales pitch which he can accept or turn down. Once he has been exposed to enough pop-ups offering such a vacation, then regular emails, printed mailings, and phone calls can often sway humans into getting hooked on an agreement with long-lasting hidden costs.

Perhaps the most tempting of the freebies you might offer someone in Tom's shoes is the week-long cruise to the Bahamas at "no cost" to him or his wife. By taking this trip, he can prove to C. J. that he is not the slave to labor she so often claims he is, and doing it without spending a dollar will prove his wise use of their financial means. The meals served on the cruise are made for kings and queens and included in the zero-cost-offer.

Add to that scuba, wind-sailing, a poolside room, six choices of live entertainment every evening, facial massages, limitless hours of wireless hookups via satellite to check emails and surf the web, and sixty-six choices of television amusement from around the world if he should get bored with everything else, and Tom will find it virtually impossible to admit he was bored.

The fine print disclaimer that comes with this exclusive package is that, in order for him to travel at no financial cost, both Tom and C. J. must agree to select three one-hour seminars to attend. While each seminar is marketing a different topic, the message is discreetly identical: "You cannot make it through life on your own." The challenges are far too global to wield on one's own and we have available today the only solutions ever proven to meet those needs.

Yes, Rail, I too have a list of the products that have failed to meet his imagined needs, yet keep Tom focused on the foolishness of waiting for tomorrow to satisfy every one of his desires. From there it is a small step to have him looking out for numero uno because, after all, who else will? If no one else will meet his desires, he had better step out and take for himself what he certainly deserves and has earned. The cruise is just the step he needs to do such a thing. Add to that the bonus of this appearing spiritual to C. J. as he takes time away from work, and you can succeed on numerous fronts at once.

As long as he remains self-focused, you can be sure that, at least for today, he is right in your hands. Be alert, but keep up the miserable work.

evalS_rekaM :-{(

From the Chat Room:

FROM: Harry@humboldt.com
Subtle or not, there is one thing he's right about. Regardless of what we think we really can't make it through life on our own.

FROM: Lilly@firstborn.edu
You're right. My Dad used to watch the *Lone Ranger*[3] as a kid and told me lots of stories about how one guy stood up for what was right. It reminded me of watching *The Mask of Zorro*[4] last night, because the idea was the same, all about one person standing up alone to fix the worst problems.

FROM:Harry@humboldt.com
But there's no such thing as a Lone Ranger or Zorro. Every one of us depends on somebody or something. The truth is that when we depend on something other than God we'll get let down. But when we rely on Him, He never lets us down.

"Has anyone by fussing before the mirror ever gotten taller by so much as an inch? If fussing can't even do that, why fuss at all? Walk into the fields and look at the wildflowers. They don't fuss with their appearance—but have you ever seen color and design quite like it? The ten best-dressed men and women in the country look shabby alongside them. If God gives such attention to the wildflowers, most of them never even seen, don't you think he'll attend to you, take pride in you, and do his best for you?

"What I'm trying to do here is get you to relax, not be so preoccupied with getting so you can respond to God's giving. People who don't know God and the way he works fuss over these things, but you know both God and how he works. Steep yourself in God-reality, God-initiative, and God-provisions. You'll find all your everyday human concerns will be met. Don't be afraid of missing out. You're my dearest friends! The Father wants to give you the very kingdom itself."

LUKE 12:25–32

Email 21

FROM: evalS_rekaM@loweryet.net
TO: Rail@hellnet.com
Subject: Blog this...Blog that...Blog, Blog, Blog
Received: 05.18.06

Rail,

Here's what they say about themselves, "Your BLOG is what you want it to be." As much as I gag upon the next word, "truly" a BLOG can provide an extremely useful forum for you to advertise the most full-blown lies you can envision and it will cost you nothing! I have taken the liberty to create a dozen blogs for you. You will be the only one entering data into the discussions and each has a different photo already attached (3 female) (3 male) (3 ages) (3 races) (6 nations). Yet you are the only one with master access to any of them.

If used wisely, you will find this a free forum in which you can share what appears to be a conversation between strangers, but every bit of it will come from your various log-on sites. You will be able to present yourself as one who cares, another who appears to be wise, one who thinks clearly, and others who are simply reporting what they see to be the truth surrounding them. At the same time, you will be in a position to claim expertise in dozens of fields, selling the identical perjuries in a mass of styles to a far-reaching gathering of idiots. I have begun to drool again even as I have described the layout to you.

The lies will be anonymous, they will be listened to, pondered, chewed on, and best of all, planted without a bit of personal effort on your part. All you need to do is lie creatively and you will have the privilege of growing the seeds of lies without many of the efforts required of so many of your predecessors.

BLOGS are fantastic FREE advertising for the building of one's life upon a lie. Don't miss out on this opportunity.

evalS_rekaM :-{(

—

Responses I received:

FROM: Cory@hobo.com
The number of free things I have supposedly won this week is crazy! If I
believed all my emails of the last week, I would have three new computers,
$100 apiece at Walmart, Kmart, and Target, a package of free growth
hormones, a getaway to Atlantic City, and 20 million pounds in Great Britain
Sterling. That's just by emails. The supposed value of junk floating around out
there via blogs is even more!

—

"But if you just use my words in Bible studies and don't work
them into your life, you are like a stupid carpenter who built his
house on the sandy beach. When a storm rolled in and the waves
came up, it collapsed like a house of cards."

MATTHEW 7:26–27

Email 22

FROM: evalS_rekaM@loweryet.net

TO: Rail@hellnet.com

Subject: "I get to got"

Received: 05-24-06

Rail,

When Tom was a little boy, one of his kindergarten classmates had a genuine problem in speaking, and another with her memory. While his parents told him repeatedly not to make fun of those who had less ability than he did, he loved making fun of Rosie. When she could not recall the simplest answer she would look at their teacher, shrug and say, "I get to got."

The brief nature of human memory is laughable isn't it? Tom forgot C. J.'s birthday last month and then their anniversary today. His busy lifestyle contributes to that. His regular attempts to do too much too often regularly overloads his system. Yet the most amusing part of it is that his forgetfulness is the one consistent habit in his life. Tom habitually forgives himself with the excuse that he simply cannot help it. He tried but he forgot. There is simply too much to do for his RAM to handle or his hard drive to store.

As the years have passed, Tom has sought to make light of each lazy stumbling goof by quoting the classmate of long ago, giving a shrug, pasting on his grin and saying, "I get to got." Those who see or hear it from him seldom might smile, but his wife, his son, and his coworkers and neighbors have ceased seeing it as anything more than it really is: an excuse often used in the attempt to explain away his own forgetfulness failure and laziness in that part of his life.

The truth of it is that Tom has enveloped himself with such a long-lasting, and often-repeated piece of fiction that he falls to it automatically. So much of the time he finds himself with no other tool to use. Add to that the irritation the habit has caused for those around him. This provides us with an exceptional opportunity to press him one step further toward hopelessness. In desperate moments like that, Tom could be ready to hear and accept almost any solution you might offer. Watch carefully. Push regularly. Spring instantly. If you miss the opportunity, do not bother to tell me, "I get to got."

evalS_rekaM :-{(

—

Those people are on a dark spiral downward. But if you think that leaves you on the high ground where you can point your finger at others, think again. Every time you criticize someone, you condemn yourself. It takes one to know one. Judgmental criticism of others is a well-known way of escaping detection in your own crimes and misdemeanors. But God isn't so easily diverted. He sees right through all such smoke screens and holds you to what you've done.

ROMANS 2:1–2

Email 23

FROM: evalS_rekaM@loweryet.net
TO: Rail@hellnet.com
Subject: The Spotlight—Same Song Next Verse
Received: 05.30.06

Rail,

As a kid, the refrain of one of the absurd songs Tom chose to memorize was, Scout Song No. 648, commonly referred to as "Nelly in the Barn." It's refrain was a string of silly repetitive words: "Same song, next verse, a little bit louder and a little bit worse." While it proved to be irritating to his father if Tom sang it loud enough and often enough, frequent repetition with great volume can be exceedingly effective for us. For example, try saying, "Health. Health. Health." The mixture of commercials for medications, news reports on the potential aid from the most recent potential surgery, and reports which seem to show the exact opposite can be useful in leading Tom down the path toward believing that G_d is totally unable and absolutely uninterested when it comes to assisting him as problems occur in his life.

Having perused Tom's database, I have observed the repeated pains in his back for which no medical personnel have been able to provide relief for him. You might well carry Tom far onto the darkened path through repeated, aggressive, even confrontational pop-ups which recognize claim to the excruciation he has lived with for twenty-two years, merely a spot of genuine time, yet eternity in his feeble mind.

Once he has focused again on his own pain, help him begin pondering once again what he might have done to earn such hatred from the opponent. You may even whisper that perhaps G_d does not really care about regular average people like Tom. He only cares about those who are important enough; who have achieved power enough; have become wealthy enough; or perhaps those who have simply earned his favor.

As you employ strings of aggressive pop-ups, never fail to keep his focus upon himself and his own pet pain. Never ever allow him to even consider the difficulties, pains, or losses others may endure. Tom worked in a camera shop during his college years and reminded every customer that focus was the key to good-looking photographs. Remind Tom that focus is the key here as well. Keep him focused on false compassion, anger, despair, and darkness and you will see quite sharply our most desired, delightful, and lascivious results.

Persistently encourage Tom to pursue a constant search for what might work better in relieving his pain than what he has already seen or tried. The endless search for relief will be a joy to observe. Constantly remind Tom that as the world changes and medicines change, he will be able to find better things for every part of his life, but that will only come to be if he dedicates himself to the pursuit of constant new desires and remedies. Do it seductively enough and eventually Tom will be longing to hear, "Things change, Tom. If you stop looking now, you will certainly be left behind and miss the cure around the corner."

As he continuously pursues such relief, encourage Tom to shift from chasing support of any kind to despairing over help not found. Attached you will find a list of contemporary lines from songs and films of all styles which will reinforce the hopelessness of trying to make it on his own.

You might even choose to send Tom the "free" DVD as a supposed promo from another wing of my office, FVRU (Free Videos Are Us), which highlights hopelessness. The title? *Nothing Really Changes.*

Keep his spotlight upon himself and his pain and you will be more loathsome than you are now.

evalS_rekaM :-{(

—

"If I were in your shoes, I'd go straight to God, I'd throw myself on the mercy of God. After all, he's famous for great and un- expected acts; there's no end to his surprises. He gives rain, for instance, across the wide earth, sends water to irrigate the fields. He raises up the down-and-out, gives firm footing to those sinking in grief. He aborts the schemes of conniving crooks, so that none of their plots come to term. He catches the know-it-alls in their conspiracies—all that intricate intrigue swept out with the trash! Suddenly they're disoriented, plunged into darkness; they can't see to put one foot in front of the other. But the down-trodden are saved by God, saved from the murderous plots, and saved from the iron fist. And so the poor continue to hope, while injustice is bound and gagged."

Job 5: 8–13

Email 24

FROM: evalS_rekam@loweryet.net
TO: Rail@hellnet.com
Subject: Mountains and Valleys
Received: 06.06.06

Rail,

Constant change can be your friend as Tom and C. J. travel. Their vacation last week in the mountains and valleys of Switzerland and their side trip from Zurich up into the mountains and the town of Davos took them through dozens of other cities, towns and villages. They climbed half a dozen mountains, finding themselves in the darkness of numerous tunnels under the mountains, and if they had closed their eyes for sixty seconds and reopened them, their surroundings at that moment would have been totally different each time as they passed from mountain to mountain and valley to valley.

It takes no especially skilled scientist or research team to see the value and power that lies in keeping them hungry for change at the same rate and with the same magnificence they thought they saw in the mountains. This is especially true now that they have returned to the valley of boredom.

Once you have helped push C. J. and Tom in that direction, you can nudge them toward the next valley with a new variety of lows as they long to recapture the mountaintop. Enhance their memory of the recent past so that it seems higher than it actually was. Consequently, their present surroundings and their everyday life will feel lower than they in fact are.

A fresh openness to temptation quite often follows as humans seek to cling to nonexistent mountaintop memories. The most consistently effortless item I have ever experienced is that of luring a human creature into thinking that it deserves the best their miserable world has to offer one hundred percent of the time. Shuffling their memories about vacations, holidays and furloughs of every kind often will lead them into becoming malcontents for life. The opportunities that lie ahead are genuinely magnificent . Do not miss them.

evalS_rekaM :-{(

Responses I received:

FROM: Adam@anet.net
The longer I have a guy on a team, the easier it is for me to coach him because he already knows the basics. It struck me here that the liar ignored one thing: the longer you walk with the Lord, the more you recognize one basic truth about God's love: your value does not lie in anything you ever do, but in what He has already done on the cross.

FROM: Katie@rpie.com
I understand the concept of how hard it is to come down from a mountaintop experience and go back to normal everyday life. That's what every fall is like for the children in the first few weeks of every school year.

FROM: Colin@@hobo.com
I recognize what you are saying, but you overlook how hard it is to stay on vacation, living out of a suitcase for a long time. I know, right now you're saying you'd like to give it a try sometime, but I do it for work. It's not all it's imagined to be.

FROM:Ryan@rpie.com
You both missed the point.

FROM: Adam@anet.net
Then what's the point?

FROM:Ryan@rpie.com
Just this. God does use us in huge ways sometimes. At other times, He gives us rest. But after that He gives us the privilege of going back to work for Him.

The danger, at least part of it anyway, isn't just in longing for the greatness of the past; far weightier is forgetting whom you're working for.

—

About eight days after saying this, he climbed the mountain to pray, taking Peter, John, and James along. While he was in prayer, the appearance of his face changed and his clothes became blinding white. At once two men were there talking with him. They turned out to be Moses and Elijah—and what a glorious appearance they made! They talked over his exodus, the one Jesus was about to complete in Jerusalem.

Meanwhile, Peter and those with him were slumped over in sleep. When they came to, rubbing their eyes, they saw Jesus in his glory and the two men standing with him. When Moses and Elijah had left, Peter said to Jesus, "Master, this is a great moment! Let's build three memorials: one for you, one for Moses, and one for Elijah." He blurted this out without thinking.

While he was babbling on like this, a light-radiant cloud enveloped them. As they found themselves buried in the cloud, they became deeply aware of God. Then there was a voice out of the cloud: "This is my Son, the Chosen! Listen to him." When the sound of the voice died away, they saw Jesus there alone. They were speechless. And they continued speechless, said not one thing to anyone during those days of what they had seen.

When they came down off the mountain the next day, a big crowd was there to meet them . . .

LUKE 9:28–37

Email 25

FROM: evalS_rekaM@loweryet.net
TO: Rail@hellnet.com
Subject: What's his crutch?
Received: 06.13.06

Rail,

Your confusion over how to best use human weakness displays the useless level of training you received before being put on the field. A recent example from Tom's own life is how only a few months ago, there was an annual celebration at the place C. J. refers to as her church (though we both know it is a crutch). The fools who succumb to and follow our enemy claim that J_s_s suffered to the point that he died but only stayed that way for a while. It is essential that you pay attention to my response on this.

The celebration of such foolishness is a great opportunity for you to take advantage of the ability Tom conceitedly believes he has to reason and think his way through everything. The way the events of the Easter weekend were described to him by a high-school buddy left him thinking of a game when his football team was behind late in the game. To everyone in the stands that night it appeared that their team had been defeated, but then a last-minute scoring drive had turned losers into winners.

Once you have him in this mindset, help him remember the times when his team had fallen behind and had been unable to recapture the lead in the game. I know you may think his memory has dumped access to those nights from earlier years in his life, but believe me when I tell you that he still cherishes those meaningless momentary victories and remembers the times his team lost.

The next time that Tom begins to consider this resurrection idea, point out to him repeatedly that losing a ballgame and dying are not all that similar. The players who lost on Friday night were unhappy when they went to sleep, but they woke up the next morning. Perhaps they were bruised and sore, but they woke up again. After all, they had not been dead, merely behind on the scoreboard. Add to that the idea that once the game was over, the losing team could not get the score to change overnight so that they were declared winners in the morning. If that could not happen for Tom's team, how could it have happened for J_s_s ?

If you can persuade Tom to think along those lines, his wife's crutch celebration weekend may prove less believable to him.

evalS_rekaM :-{(

—

Responses I received:

FROM: Kim@anet.net
Comparing Jesus' death and resurrection to losing a ball game? That's incredibly shallow. I don't know anybody who could think like that.

FROM: Cory@hobo.com
I don't know of anybody who would say it that bluntly, but it seems to me that each of us cling to ideas about God that we use every day. We try to keep Him in a box (maybe even a really big box) so we can understand Him. But the truth is that we will never fully comprehend the depth of God's love or the amazing cost He was willing to pay for our salvation. If you want to call accepting that gift a crutch, then I have one.

FROM: Katie@rpie.com
Me too. So does everybody who comes to God via Christ's sacrifice on the cross and his return to living in his resurrection. Without that we have no hope at all.

—

After the Sabbath, as the first light of the new week dawned, Mary Magdalene and the other Mary came to keep vigil at the tomb. Suddenly the earth reeled and rocked under their feet as God's angel came down from heaven, came right up to where they were standing. He rolled back the stone and then sat on it. Shafts of lightning blazed from him. His garments shimmered snow-white. The guards at the tomb were scared to death. They were so frightened, they couldn't move.

The angel spoke to the women: "There is nothing to fear here. I know you're looking for Jesus, the One they nailed to the cross. He is not here. He was raised, just as he said. Come and look at the place where he was placed.

"Now, get on your way quickly and tell his disciples, 'He is risen from the dead. He is going on ahead of you to Galilee. You will see him there.' That's the message."

The women, deep in wonder and full of joy, lost no time in leaving the tomb. They ran to tell the disciples . . .

MATTHEW 28:1–8

Email 26

FROM: evalS_rekaM@loweryet.net
TO: Rail@hellnet.com
Subject: The MESS of Movies
Received: 06.18.06

Rail,

I can't believe that it has taken you half a human century to accept and implement the teachings of your multimedia programming trainers. The impact of moving images has exceeded all our initial projections. In house, the potentials are referred to as MESS, since we seek to influence people mentally, emotionally, socially and spiritually every time they go see a movie. While we continue to strive toward full mental control of humans, we are not yet fully functional in that area. Nonetheless, our findings indicate that if you can build a bridge between the movie and Tom, all four aspects of his persona will be influenced since these parts of a human's life are so intertwined. You will find examples attached below of how MESS has worked for us in the past.

M—Mental impact. Mental impact is really focused on overflowing, overfilling and dulling. We have found that the more times we can get humans to observe gruesome events, the more we are able to dull their response to other's needs. Whether it be Liar's Poker ® in 1999, or the simply titled television show Crime Stories ®, the higher the number of crimes you can get Tom exposed to, the better the chances are that he will begin to look past truly nasty events. A prime example is Guatemala. Over the years people there have seen so many civilians slain, that dead bodies are regularly left in the street. Murder has become so second nature to them in some areas that charges are not even filed against the one known to have killed their spouse.

E—Emotional. In terms of emotional input, fear in theaters is perhaps the simplest. Quick movements and bright lights which follow an extended period of darkness or shadows and either high or low-pitched noises of great volume can startle people. While such a combination of events alone can be useful, it has been shown to be far more destructive if the supposed cause for the string of events is non-human. It does seem that when Tom believes he is not in control, fear is his general reaction. While he seeks to cover that up with anger, most of the time it is because he is afraid of what might happen next.

S—Social. The social impact of our efforts has been spoken of as non-existent, but the fact that the new movies last year earned over $8.8 billion alone shows that our influence socially is great. Why you may ask? For the industry to earn that, millions of people had to give money to view the films initially. Then over 66,000 DVD versions were made available by just one of the marketers out there so that the terror of the in-theater experience could be repeated at home.

Our frustration was immense several generations ago when, in 1918, all theaters were closed in America due to the influenza spreading like wildfire through the nation. Since cable television, DVDs, and satellite dishes had yet to be invented, our ability to influence people mentally, emotionally and socially was reduced at least in the short run. Feel free to read the *New York Time* article from October 5, 2005, *Deadly 1918 Epidemic Linked to Bird Flu,* Scientists say which describes this in further detail. You can find it at http://www.nytimes.com/2005/10/05/health/05cnd-flu.html.

S—Spiritual. When it comes to spiritual influence, we have blatantly stolen a clip from a film to be released in the summer of 2007 and are attaching it for your download and preview here. At this point, the title is undecided, but we are pushing for the adoption of the title *TRANSFORMERS* ® as a computerized remake of a cartoon from twenty years ago. The message is more powerful accompanied by the image. The language they have agreed to use is important nonetheless and stated below:

> Before time began, there was a cube. We know not where it comes from, only that it holds the power to create worlds and fill them with life. That is how our race was born. For a time we lived in harmony, but like a great power, some wanted it for good; others for evil.

And so began the war, a war that ravaged our planet until it was consumed by death. And the cube was lost to the far reaches of space. We scattered across the galaxy.[5]

In addition to seeking to add temptation to a variety if sins, it is our hope that regardless of the motives of both the director and producer, this opening clip could draw people away from the idea that G_d created a thing and will instead reinforce the idea that life is far too complicated to be explained by the simple answer to which some still cling.

Knowing how much Tom likes to go to the movies, it would be wise for you to review your earlier training regarding multimedia and seek more ways to use the movies to your advantage.

evalS_ rekaM :-{(

From the Chat Room:

FROM: Thatch@akson.org
I look forward to seeing the film when it's released. If what they say about it's beginning is true, it could be a sly way to get people to think about everything existing because of a force somewhere out there that was itself created by something else, leaving God out of the whole picture.

FROM: Jack@west1.net
I see what you mean. I plan to go see it too. This whole thing helps me realize once more that such a claim is ridiculous. God made everything. He is the only one with the ability to create a world or create life.

FROM: Harry@humboldt.com
Regardless of what either of you say, it's important for us not to get sucked in. We need to carefully evaluate whether what we see is true or not.

Pilate went back into the palace and called for Jesus. He said, "Are you the 'King of the Jews?'"

Jesus answered, "Are you saying this on your own, or did others tell you this about me?"

Pilate said, "Do I look like a Jew? Your people and your high priests turned you over to me. What did you do?"

"My kingdom," said Jesus, "doesn't consist of what you see around you. If it did, my followers would fight so that I wouldn't be handed over to the Jews. But I'm not that kind of king, not the world's kind of king."

Then Pilate said, "So, are you a king or not?"

Jesus answered, "You tell me. Because I am King, I was born and entered the world so that I could witness to the truth. Everyone who cares for truth, who has any feeling for the truth, recognizes my voice."

Pilate said, "What is truth?" . . .

JOHN 18:33–38

Email 27

FROM: evalS_rekam@loweryet.net
TO: Rail@hellnet.com
Subject: Free Slave
Received: 07.06.06

Rail,

You have every reason to exult and rejoice. Your successful lowering Tom's holiness performance tonight leaves me to drooling in the anticipation of his arrival. Following the celebration of the supposed liberty and freedom of the provincial dwelling he calls his home country, Tom attempted to direct his motorized vehicle to the place that he, his spouse, and their son reside. His detention following the OMVUI does indeed give you the opportunity to assist Tom in totally losing his ever-shrinking self-esteem.

To be most effective here, you will need to repeatedly remind Tom of the results of his late-night celebration of the claimed freedom of the people of his nation especially considering the fact that he had nothing to do with making it so. Replay for Tom again and again how he had allowed himself to enjoy the consummation of various levels of alcoholic beverages with the result being one of drunkenness thus far unmatched or survived by anyone else in his generation.

Given the effect of the beverages upon him, Tom was not able to steer his means of transportation perfectly or even acceptably. In spite of his foolhardy level of merrymaking and over the objection of friends, he attempted driving his vehicle home. While choosing a speed which he deemed slow, secure and subdued, he allowed his car to steer itself first into a ditch and then into a tree.

While we are saddened that the incident did not claim Tom's life so that we could indeed claim him as our slave, be encouraged that the penalties Tom faces as a result will, if properly nourished and encouraged, cause shame which will thus aid his spiral further down and further in. Twist the effects of phone calls and e-mails, which he receives from family members so that he does not understand their genuine relief that he himself was not hurt. Then hinder an accurate recollection of events and offer instead the painful memory of the death of his own father when his father's friend had driven in a more or less equivalent event.

Do not neglect the belittling of tools available for his use in recovering from this event which have too often proven helpful in steering others away from such a style of life. Most certainly you must steer him in any direction other than the images of grace and forgiveness. Seize this moment. Cause this poor choice to lead toward the feeling we find so delicious: Guilt.

For Tom's homeland, that night was a celebration of freedom, but if used in a timely manner, the fourth of July can be drawn on to remind Tom that he is a slave to alcohol who is a hopeless slave who is doomed to fail.

evalS_rekaM :-{(

___

Responses I received:

FROM: Cory@hobo.com
I lost a friend who was driving drunk. My best friend. I could have stopped him and kept his keys and driven him home myself. But I didn't. I feel guilty about it each time I remember it.

FROM: Kim@anet.net
It's true that you didn't drive for your buddy. But you didn't get him there to begin with. It was his own regular choice to do what was wrong that cost him, not yours.

FROM: Ryan@rpie.com
When someone gets so self-focused that they don't care what it costs to get drunk or make more meth or whatever their habit is, they cost everybody around them. The comfort and hope we can have when we go through anything like that is that God is bigger than anything we face. Anything.

—

By entering through faith into what God has always wanted to do for us—set us right with him, make us fit for him—we have it all together with God because of our Master Jesus. And that's not all: We throw open our doors to God and discover at the same moment that he has already thrown open his door to us. We find ourselves standing where we always hoped we might stand—out in the wide open spaces of God's grace and glory, standing tall and shouting our praise.

There's more to come: We continue to shout our praise even when we're hemmed in with troubles, because we know how troubles can develop passionate patience in us, and how that patience in turn forges the tempered steel of virtue, keeping us alert for whatever God will do next. In alert expectancy such as this, we're never left feeling shortchanged. Quite the contrary—we can't round up enough containers to hold everything God generously pours into our lives through the Holy Spirit!

ROMANS 5:1–5

Email 28

From: evalS_rekaM@loweryet.net
To: Rail@hellnet.com
Subject: Arrogant Self-Confidence
Received: 07.13.06

Rail,

Before you change your focus again, I must stress once more the importance
and benefits which your choice of words can provide you. In light of the fact
that Tom's legal counsel was able to find a loophole for the charges brought
against him, Tom walked away with merely a bare minimal financial penalty.
Thus in order to maintain even the slightest use of those events, you need to
remind yourself constantly of the usefulness of encouraging Tom to keep his
focus solely on himself.

It will not be as difficult as you might think to persuade Tom to become
arrogantly confident once again. It is quite likely that continuously reminding
him of the value of his skills to his employer, his family, his community, and of
course to the world at large, will do the trick. Add to that the ever-growing list
of those who, by his standard are idiots. They do not have cell phones, have
no clue what a blog or Trojan horse might be, do not receive email and, in
fact, are so barbarian that they do not even own a computer or Palm Pilot ®.
Given his obvious superiority in these things, there can be no doubt that those
surrounding him are worthless low-life human beings who are not worthy of his
time, his efforts, or his finances.

I hope you have begun to grasp the stupidity and arrogance that accompany
Tom's perspective of his own self worth. Due to your previous failures to
use this series of events to draw him closer, noise is rising from those below
me that you need to interchange the tools used to increase his self-focus.
Words from his boss, clients, and even C. J. can be offered on their part as
encouragements and used by you as self-focus drivers. If you do it well, self-

reliance for Tom will become nothing more than his taking one solid step after
another into quicksand from which there is seldom any return.

evalS_rekaM :-{(

—

Love God all you saints, God takes care of all who stay close to
him. He pays back in full those arrogant enough to go it alone.

PSALM 31:23

Email 29

FROM: evalS_rekaM@loweryet.net
TO: Rail@hellnet.com
Subject: Buy now! Tomorrow will be too late!
Received 07.18.06

Rail,

You fail to grasp the faultiness of the assumption that age and wisdom are linked. Do not even consider shifting the blame for these events to me. I fully understand the language selected by our foe on numerous occasions, yet it has nothing to do with the vast evidence within our most recent update entries. One more birthday does not make your prey any less susceptible. Reiterate the consequences suffered from the choices he made earlier in life. Statistically, we have seen this as a convenient implement for use in leading our prey down the road of hopelessness. This has been experienced by so many middle-aged men where the simple ages of forty and fifty have proven themselves to be efficient in leading humans to that which they shamefully title depression.

Tom's desire to ignore his fiftieth birthday is an indicator of his potential weakness in this area. He does not view himself as having reached any goals of lasting value. For years, Tom held onto the naïve notion that he should be recognized as valuable, regardless of the standards, which others applied. Remind him of that repeatedly each time he considers the goals he pursued earlier in life and the utter failure he has had in reaching any of them.

With their oldest son, Jeffrey, now out of the house and on his own, today is the perfect day to highlight the quantity of time Tom has pursued self-gratifying success. Then highlight the time he has lost with his son. Tom gave so little to his eldest son. Is it any wonder that Jeffrey no longer has time he wishes to invest in his father?

Tom has done much the same with C. J. Lead him to ask if a reason exists why this wife of many years would have one bit of desire to continue in this relationship. With all of this being true, is there really any reason he should even take one more breath? Tom's failure is complete and all based upon the definition of value that he allowed us to plant and water so many years ago. So relentlessly tell him again him of the strength and stamina he thought he had and the mentally keen edge which he no longer seems to be able to log onto. The numbers of forty and fifty can be superb tools for just such non-celebrations.

Do not disregard this counsel. The next notification in which I am required to attach such a warning to your email will be your last.

evalS_rekaM :-{(

—

Responses I received:

From: Colin@hobo.com
That is one of the biggest lies I ever dealt with myself. "Colin, you're 40 now. Your best days are certainly behind you. Not much point in going on." Yet in the last 10, the Lord has helped me sort out and deal with many of the things I allowed to consume my time earlier. Every day God permits me to see just a bit more of what it means to follow Him.

From: Adam@anet.net
I look back today and am grateful for times God has helped me keep my focus off of what looked good at the moment and refocus so often on the great things he has planned for me.

―

By an act of faith, Joseph, while dying, prophesied the exodus of Israel, and made arrangements for his own burial. By an act of faith, Moses' parents hid him away for three months after his birth. They saw the child's beauty, and they braved the king's decree. By faith, Moses, when grown, refused the privileges of the Egyptian royal house.

By an act of faith, Israel walked through the Red Sea on dry ground. The Egyptians tried it and drowned. By faith, the Israelites marched around the walls of Jericho for seven days, and the walls fell flat. By an act of faith, Rahab, the Jericho harlot, welcomed the spies and escaped the destruction that came on those who refused to trust God.

HEBREWS 11:22–24

I could go on and on, but I've run out of time. There are so many more.... We have stories of those who were stoned, sawed in two, murdered in cold blood; stories of vagrants wandering the earth in animal skins, homeless, friendless, powerless—the world didn't deserve them!—making their way as best they could on the cruel edges of the world.

HEBREWS 11:32–38

Not one of these people, even though their lives of faith were exemplary, got their hands on what was promised. God had a better plan for us: that their faith and our faith would come together to make one completed whole, their lives of faith not complete apart from ours.

HEBREWS 39–40

FROM: evalS_rekaM@loweryet.net
TO: Rail@hellnet.com
Subject: Juggling A Wet Fleece
Received: 07.24.06

Rail,

You reported that Tom has learned to juggle. While he claims it to be relaxing, it is little more than a reflection of how he lives the majority of his life. He seeks to do so many things at the same time that he is not able to do any of them well. So, to keep them all going, he rushes from project 1 to project 2, putting out enough fires to keep each one afloat, then he rushes on to the next thing he is juggling.

While that is commonly seen among people who can do more than one thing well, here is the beauty of it: if J_s_s really was fully G_d and man at the same time, how could he possibly do much more than nod and smile and wave when humans talk to him in what they call prayer? Take a look at Ask ®, Google®, or any other search engine you care to use, enter the word "prayer" and you will find somewhere in the neighborhood of 2,000,000 possible websites that describe it or give statistical evidence regarding it.

One of those sites recently claimed over 175,000 hits by individuals praying as a result of their contact with that site. If you can steer Tom in that direction, show him the largest number of supposed prayers possible, then raise the question of how G_d could possibly be bombarded with such an enormous number of prayers in a day and make sense of them. If that is not enough to turn Tom away from this idea of praying, whisper that if G_d received that many prayers, his only possible response would be dumping them in the trash or at best, juggling them in the same way Tom claims to have found a release for the tension in his life.

I wrote to you several months ago regarding Tom seeking to keep many balls in the air at the same time. The principle here is the same. With all that he accomplishes, Tom gives only a little attention to each project. Even if God were as great as he claims, with so many requests, does it make any sense at all to think G_d could listen to Tom? Even if he could, what makes Tom think G_d would listen to him or help him before he did all the others?

If he begins to fancy the idea that G_d has heard and answered him, encourage Tom to ask again, just to be sure he got the answer right. My point is to keep Tom juggling to relax. Consistently remind him of G_d juggling Tom's meager attempt at praying with all the others that are sent his way.

evalS_ rekaM :-{(

From the Chat Room:

FROM: Lilly@firstborn.edu
I used to wonder if God wouldn't hear me better if only I prayed louder and if I wouldn't stand a better chance of getting what I wanted if I simply asked for it more often. And if I did get an answer to prayer, I would be sure I got it straight from God, so I would ask again, just in slightly different terms. Then I was reminded that God never said I needed to have a magic formula for praying and I didn't need exact phrases for Him to hear me better. And when I didn't know exactly what to pray for, the Holy Spirit went before the throne and said what I just couldn't find the right words for.

FROM: Jack@west1.net
You're right, but prayer isn't just about asking. It's also about listening For God's answer. I've always been thankful that He doesn't get tired of listening to me and answering me, even if I don't catch His answer the first time.

Gideon said to God, "If this is right, if you are using me to save Israel as you've said, then look: I'm placing a fleece of wool on the threshing floor. If dew is on the fleece only, but the floor is dry, then I know that you will use me to save Israel, as you said."

That's what happened. When he got up early the next morning, he wrung out the fleece—enough dew to fill a bowl with water!

Then Gideon said to God, "Don't be impatient with me, but let me say one more thing. I want to try another time with the fleece. But this time let the fleece stay dry, while the dew drenches the ground."

God made it happen that very night. Only the fleece was dry while the ground was wet with dew.

JUDGES 6:36–40

Email 31

To: evalS_rekaM@loweryet.net
From: Rail@hellnet.com
Subject: So Sad . . .
Received: 07.30.06

Rail,

Whenever anyone around Tom goes through a disaster or catastrophe, remind him of the letter he received from his father while he was in college. Remind him that, before the days of email, difficult as it was, as a freshman in college, he had written home asking for money when he had squandered his savings on pizza and nights out with his buddies, resulting in being flat broke. The response he received from home came immediately:

> Dear Son,
> No Mon . . . No Fun?
> So Sad . . . Too Bad!
> Your Dad

While it was only a petty need, when anyone near him aches for any reason, remind him of that experience and embellish the pain he felt. The sense of rejection, panic, and anger he still carries bundled up thirty years later. Keep his focus upon himself instead of on those with genuine needs.

Both can serve as tailor-made worms. Past tragedies can be used to water his anger, and if tweaked, current events can prove themselves to be just as useful, such as the untimely, unexpected death of C. J.'s friend, Anne. C. J. and Anne got to know each other at work several years ago. They both began on the same day and found themselves working on project after project together on the same team. Today, though she was ten years younger than C. J., Anne was killed in a car accident, and while everyone else walked away unscratched, Anne died at the site.

C. J. was so utterly shocked that now is the perfect moment for you to challenge the ideas she has so easily adopted regarding G_d, especially the thought that what G_d does is right, whether it makes any sense or not. Lead C. J. to consider the time of the event. Clearly, Anne's came far too early, especially when one considers the crimes and lifestyles of those who live on. http://www.lonelyplanet.com, http://rtigroupaligarh.blogspot.com, and numerous other sites can help you list for her the many lawbreaker and others she considers as low-life criminals who continue to live. Add to this list of concern, anger, and anxiety the blunt question of how Anne's husband will ever be able to raise and provide for their four children on his own.

Work hastily here. This can be an opportunity to hook both Tom and C. J. if executed properly. With a focus on pain, personal loss, and injustice, you can help them increase their doubts regarding there being any true meaning of life. Shuffle the cards these moments of pain occur and always deal from the bottom of the deck. Whenever one suffers, foster their partner, in effect, to say, "So sad . . . Too Bad!"

evalS_rekaM :-{(

—

Take my side, God—I'm getting kicked around, stomped on every day. Not a day goes by but somebody beats me up; They make it their duty to beat me up. When I get really afraid I come to you in trust. I'm proud to praise God; fearless now, I trust in God. What can mere mortals do?

PSALM 56:1–4

Email 32

From: evalS_rekaM@loweryet.net
To: Rail@hellnet.com
Subject: Gatorade ®, Mountain Dew ®, or Aquafina ®?
Received: 08.06.06

Rail,

Your causing Tom to fall flat on his back, hit his head, and pass out in the mall was a despicable event. He has, at least temporarily, been wooed away from the aged tool of drunkenness and your attempts to woo him toward any of the highly addictive and misery-providing drugs have all been unsuccessful. Even so, you have made exquisite use of the numerous cold beverages when he tripped and fell in the mall. As he ran into the mall to grab some pop having him literally trip on his own shoelaces was shamefully ingenious.

During his hustling through the mall on the way to the other six things he had committed to do on his day off, Tom paused long enough to try to select the one beverage that would quench his unending thirst. As he did, Tom slipped, and fell down, briefly viewing both floor and ceiling before passing out for several minutes. When he regained his consciousness, staring down on Tom were machines dispensing an entire aisle of choices with meaningless titles that had each been designed to woo him away from all other beverages.

As he laid there, Tom pondered which would provide the energy he needed, quench his thirst, accelerate muscular development, and be the most appealing for him to be seen consuming. A few moments later, he realized that none of them could do all those things, left the mall and went home with the most throbbing headache he had ever experienced.

Every time the opportunity presents itself, remind Tom that he has never experienced anything that truly quenched his thirst. With that being the case, it is only logical that if nothing can deal with his physical thirst, then nothing could have been developed or marketed to do away with this thirst he has felt spiritually.

Add to this the reminder that Tom should call his attorney tomorrow morning, or better yet, tonight, as he contemplates filing the $6,000,000 lawsuit for the negligence of the mall owners, nearby stores and passers-by who did nothing to assist him. Collectively their negligence must have contributed to Tom's fall and each should therefore be forced to recompense him for his own clumsiness. Hah! There are moments in which there is no end to the benefits we reap in the little things of life.

It has indeed been a pleasure for me to observe your applying the results of a small fall to lead Tom on the road to temptation toward a larger one. Keep him thirsty and searching for something to quench it.

evalS_rekaM :-{(

Responses I received:

FROM: Colin@hobo.com
A friend of mine in Switzerland once asked me if I knew what Americans were best known for. When I said no, he asked me who I was suing this week. We're best known for a string of lawsuits as we try to get something for nothing!

FROM: Ryan@rpie.com
That drives me crazy too. But it also makes me wonder what we think it will take to really make us happy.

The woman said, "Sir, you don't even have a bucket to draw with, and this well is deep. So how are you going to get this 'living water?' Are you a better man than our ancestor Jacob, who dug this well and drank from it, he and his sons and livestock, and passed it down to us?"

Jesus said, "Everyone who drink s this water will get thirsty again and again. Anyone who drinks the water I give will never thirst—not ever. The water I give will be an artesian spring within, gushing fountains of endless life."

JOHN 4:11–14

Email 33

From: evalS_rekaM@loweryet.net
To: Rail@hellnet.com
Subject: Living at the Fair
Received: 08.13.06

Rail,

Your recent report included Tom's trip to the State Fair. Here is a trio of tools at your disposal: the Merry-Go-Round, the Ferris wheel, and the Scrambler. While each of these is an ancient ride in comparison to the current day, they remind Tom of his childhood years and the entertainment he longed for every time he went to the fair as a little boy.

Even today the Merry-Go-Round remains a popular choice. It serves as a splendid illustration of circular decision-making. To assist Tom in beginning the circular thought-pattern, when Tom thinks in what he deems to be a careful and prudent manner, suggest that he begin once again to mull over whether or not he genuinely likes the color they just painted his den. While green was not his favorite color yesterday, might it not be appropriate to have that room be the same color as the fresh life growing behind their house which he so enjoys?

On the other hand, considering that life is fresh and the paint is dry and stale, wouldn't the choice of green paint be a mere mockery of anything, which is genuinely alive? Couldn't the very walls surrounding Tom act as reminders that the growth which is yet to come will be followed by snow and ice which will cover the green of his back yard in a few short months? Yet when the seasons change once more, he will witness the spring all over again, but the green of the trees and grass will not live to tell the tale next year either. So the green walls will merely act as endless reminders of the fleeting nature of what he likes, over and over again, invoking an endless circle of aspirations that come and go quickly, just like the Merry-Go-Round.

The Ferris wheel is an equally useful portrait of the highs and lows of life. Your creature, Tom, can regularly evaluate his personal worth based upon the highs and lows of everyday existence. While celebrating birthdays and anniversaries can be times of disgusting joy regarding the accomplishments which a human believes he or she has achieved, such events can equally serve as periods in which the Ferris Wheel rotates to the bottom and your human then realize all the things they have not done. Do everything that is at your disposal to keep the times of self-acclaimed success to a minimum if they occur at all. However, if such things do come to pass in Tom's life, be sure to lead him to reflect on the opportunities he did not recognize until it was too late. As his age increases, the checklist of things Tom could have done will no doubt increase. The longer you can help him consider what could have been, the longer the wheel will get stuck at the bottom of its rotation.

My personal favorite of the images from the fairgrounds though, is the Scrambler. It offers itself as a valuable implement to throw panic into the most calm and regular low-key life a human creature might seek. While the seats they occupy on the Scrambler do not collide, the threat that they will is unending. Add to that the speed of the scramble of Tom's age. The result is quite often that a man like Tom will lose his ability to steer clear of confusion and fear, so seek out confusion and fear in as many ways as you can produce them, thus keeping them a constant part of Tom's existence. If Tom has nothing else to which he can cling, the likelihood of his accepting guidance from anyone increases and the opportunity for you to speak and for him to listen rises.

Keep him on the hopeless rides that will take him nowhere. You will rejoice. He will despair.

rekaM_evalS :-{(

—

. . . People with their minds set on you, you keep completely whole, Steady on their feet, because they keep at it and don't quit. Depend on God and keep at it because in the Lord God you have a sure thing . . .

Email 34

From: evalS_rekaM@loweryet.net
To: Rail@hellnet.com
Subject: TIVO ® or TIME
Received: 08.18.06

Rail,

TIVO ®, the new device for parents to block what their children see on television is futile. To consider it even possible to use such a simple electronic device to stifle the source of loathsome images or to prevent exposing their children to violence, offensive language, or luring sexual enticements is not all C. J. hopes it will be for them. For years now, she has been attempting to block us out, but we have continuously widened the range of existing tools to sidestep the most recent software. Her supposed care for the well-being of their son, Jeffrey, has betrayed her. Especially with his no longer living at home, C. J. really has so little input into his life, and with Jeffrey living outside of her grip, he gets closer to being in our grip each day.

When I take breaks and want a good laugh, I tune in to observe C. J.'s dependence upon outside tools. It really is quite humorous. The only software with which we have experienced genuine difficulty is limiting or preventing the amount of time given by a parent to their child. Whenever C. J. devoted time to be with Jeffrey, she possessed a massive block-out capability. Even though Jeffrey is now out of the house, and consistently pretends he does not hear anything his parents say, that sacrifice of C. J.'s time has been a block that has befuddled our lowest offices.

An example of such a sacrifice is the one Tom made for his son Jeffrey when he took an entire day away from work. We find it equally confounding and despicable. Seeing that Jeffrey's father cared enough about him to make a sacrifice of that nature blocked us out as well. On those rare occasions, Jeffrey consistently listened to what his father had to tell him. The act of taking time really told Jeffrey a great deal more than anything else Tom ever sought to teach him.

Be grateful that both Tom and C. J. swallowed the fallacy that electronic devices such as TIVO ® are providing a tool to supplant the need for sharing any of their personal time. Human parents regularly allow themselves to become so busy that sharing their time with their children is inconvenient. Hence, with regards to TIVO ® or time, keep them investing their time in buying tools like TIVO ® and you will have far less to fight.

rekaM_evalS :-{(

⸺

Responses I received:

FROM: Kim@anet.net
It would certainly be easier to let somebody else raise our children. Between the two of them they demand so much and then want me to quit telling them what to do.

FROM: Ryan@rpie.com
I know what you mean. But I remember waking my Dad to tell him I dented the car in a big way on prom night. He only said two things. "Did anybody get hurt?" When I told him no one had, he said, "Well, it's just a dent. Don't worry about it." I don't think anybody else would have been so easy on me when something bad had just happened. It made me more willing to listen to him when he said I did something wrong.

⸺

God brings death and God brings life, brings down to the grave and raises up. God brings poverty and God brings wealth; he lowers, he also lifts up. He puts poor people on their feet again; he rekindles burned-out lives with fresh hope, restoring dignity and respect to their lives—a place in the sun! For the very structures of earth are God's; he has laid out his operations on a firm foundation. He protectively cares for his faithful friends, step by step, but leaves the wicked to stumble in the dark. No one makes it in this life by sheer muscle! . . .

I Samuel 2: 6–9

Email 35

FROM: evalS_rekaM@loweryet.net
TO: Rail@hellnet.com
Subject: The Reflective Restatement of Repetition
Received: 08.24.06

Rail,

You need not be clear. You need not be deep. You need not speak one word of truth if you will simply follow my advice here: Repetition is an indispensable tool. Our most recent studies give every indication that if you simply imply in an interview that all who consume ice cream regularly will live longer, the assertion will appear foolish. However, if you then plant a newspaper article which quotes a nonexistent medical study which reaches the conclusion that in some cases those eating ice cream more than once a week lived an average of 2.5 years longer, a few will believe it to be true. Since repetition is a crucial device for you to use, you should then follow the second round of stories with the results of an independent study which you plant in a mass mailing, a commercial, or any other place or time where Tom is likely to see or hear it and he will now have been exposed to the same nonsense three times and because the recurrence of lies has been shown to be provide an influential instrument, you must not neglect its use.

The value in such a tool is that you need not be meticulous about being creative. Mere repetition will suffice. It makes little difference whatsoever what you choose to say. While a particular lie may seem to be ineffective in Tom's life today, most often all it really needs is to be embellished just a bit differently. Changing the flavor of poison never removes its deadliness, but it does provide additional opportunities for the poison to be desired and then devoured.

While my counsel to you is sound, the truth is that if a human has decided not to listen, repetition alone will not succeed. G_d continues to offer to humans the opportunity to call out to Him and has promised He will answer them and be with them. So if Tom has the tiniest inclination to buy your lie, dressing it differently often enough can facilitate the selling of the lie.

Lest you think this is not so, please note that it is exactly what I have done with you in this communication regarding repetition. While I enjoy belittling you by repeating such introductory lessons, my point has not been that I think you did not understand me the first time I expressed the importance of using repetitions to increase your likelihood of successfully sucking Tom into the lie of the day. This email is merely the use of the tool to demonstrate to you that when an idea is repeated often enough, the probability of your victory rises.

rekaM_evalS :-{(

—

Responses I received:

FROM: Adam@anet.net
After coaching for a few years I have begun to see this in a new way. To help players grow I need to find several ways to show them the same thing. Some catch on when I draw a play out. For another group, simply telling them works. Others need to actually run the play before they understand what I'm trying to tell them. I guess that's what God did. He actually ran the play when His Son went to the cross.

—

. . . by giving himself completely at the Cross, actually dying for you, Christ brought you over to God's side and put your lives together, whole and holy in his presence. You don't walk away from a gift like that! You stay grounded and steady in that bond of trust, constantly tuned in to the Message, careful not to be distracted or diverted. There is no other Message—just this one. Every creature under heaven gets this same Message. I, Paul, am a messenger of this Message.

COLOSSIANS 1:22–23

Email 36

FROM: evalS_rekaM@loweryet.net
TO: Rail@hellnet.com
Subject: Phil: The Ruler of Heck
Date: 09.06.06

Rail,

The comic strip you attached to the most recent report was chosen well. It was ingenious for Dilbert's boss to have hired "Phil, the Ruler of Heck"[6] to play the role of Devil's advocate in the meeting. Phil's response of announcing his purpose by saying that he was not certified to do "Devil Work" and then claiming that the best he could do was to roll his eyes and be sarcastic, was truly cunning. But we laughed out loud when, only moments later in the meeting, as the boss said that they would move on, Phil interrupted him in the most uncomplimentary manner, saying, "Oh yeah, this is a good time to move on! The classic reaction from the typical human was then to smile and chuckle at the very idea of Natas being one dressed in a red suit and causing trouble because it was how he earned enough to pay expenses.

The value of this for us lies in several places:

First, the name Phil is common and not Satanic-sounding. How could our leader further down actually possess the name of a regular person?

Secondly, the utterly foolish appearance of the "devil suit" is another cunning system of belittling the thought of our master even existing, and if he does not exist, how could he be involved in tempting? Beyond that, if he does not exist, then the eternal existence of punishment must certainly not be a possibility either.

Third, he is the ruler of heck, not of damnation or hell, but of heck, and minimizing the impact of the name is marvelous!

Fourth, the title "Devil's Advocate" is a phrase commonly used among humans with other meaning and therefore redefining it in such a manner adds to the impact.

Fifth, considering that Phil had to be hired by the company to carry out the task, minimizes his importance and mentally lessens any widespread impact we might have if we do exist. If each company had to hire such an employee, it is surely possible, then, that Tom's employer has not done so. If that is the case, then the very possibility of his being tempted is thus eliminated.

Sixth, encouraging Tom to laugh at the idea of temptation unlocks and opens doors to us. If Tom will laugh at temptation being spoofed, it is such a minor step to having him surrender to temptation.

Phil, the ruler of Heck, is not the real story, yet if you can keep Tom laughing at Phil, your task will be easier than if he takes temptation seriously.

rekaM_evalS :-{(

Responses I received:

FROM: Ryan@rpie.com
The "Ruler of Heck" made me begin to wonder what other things I have been placated into laughing at it instead of recognizing them for what they really are.

FROM: Katie@rpie.com
I think we will battle that all our lives here because as long as we are here we will be fighting Satan and all his tactics. Getting us to see evil so often that we get dulled to it is simply one of them.

FROM: Ryan@rpie.com
The good part for us in a life filled with such confrontations is that God knows what we're going through and is bigger than any of them.

FROM: Katie@rpie.com
Add to that the fact that He is there with us 24/7, no matter what we face. We need to keep ourselves from falling asleep spiritually. But every one of my little students would tell you that they know Mom or Dad will answer if they cry at night. Even if Satan has lulled us to sleep, God will be there when we wake up and cry His name. It's not too late!

—

. . .Without all the paraphernalia of the law code, sin looked pretty dull and lifeless, and I went along without paying much attention to it. But once sin got its hands on the law code and decked itself out in all that finery, I was fooled, and fell for it. The very command that was supposed to guide me into life was cleverly used to trip me up, throwing me headlong. So sin was plenty alive, and I was stone dead. But the law code itself is God's good and common sense, each command sane and holy counsel.

I can already hear your next question: "Does that mean I can't even trust what is good [that is, the law]? Is good just as dangerous as evil?" No again! Sin simply did what sin is so famous for doing: using the good as a cover to tempt me to do what would finally destroy me. By hiding within God's good commandment, sin did far more mischief than it could ever have accomplished on its own.

ROMANS 7:8–13

Email 37

FROM: evalS_rekaM@loweryet.net
TO: Rail@hellnet.com
Subject: 9-11
Received: 09.10.06

Rail,

9-11-01. Some humans continue to seek to record that day as no more significant than any other day in their history. Do not deceive yourself. Every piece of software currently at our disposal evaluates the string of events preceding, during and following the September 11 attacks as tragic. Yet while such loathsome memories flood the minds of millions of human beings, as slaves of Natas, we delight.

The hijacks and crashes of aircraft on 9-11 have offered us two useful tools. They are merely continuations of plants for which we laid seed generations ago.

Tool #1: Hatred is one such plant. Political disagreements over the wars that have followed, have proven themselves to be a well-designed string of events for us in this regard.

Whenever people face disaster, they tend to join ranks. Difficult as a joined group of humans can appear to be, they are not insurmountable. The most efficient application of this principle has been that of coaxing them into blaming a variety of enemies for the disaster, and the more the better, for if they cannot agree regarding who is to blame for their tragedy, they will divide themselves back into smaller groups, each seeking revenge and fighting with others over where to get the money to fund their "perfect" revenge. The more you observe it, the more quickly you will realize that hatred by humans as a group separates them, making them loathe each other. Instead, use every tragedy possible to stir up even more hatred.

Tool #2: Fear. Even though the tragedy of 9-11 is five years in their past, it can be used to rekindle the worry that the same thing could happen at any time. In even its lowest level, those swallowed by such panic are held at bay and very unlikely to stand against us in any way. If they can be convinced that cowering in the corner is the only option at their disposal, at a bare minimum they will not be on the battlefield standing against us.

Another marvelous benefit for us regarding fear is that once it is established, fear quickly forms into a habit. The most minor event of a day can be used to alarm the human to whom you are assigned. Repeat it often enough and alarm turns into panic, which in turn, becomes hopelessness. This will happen more frequently if you can convince them that they must do everything on their own to make it through life, even seeking to earn the favor of G_d. Trap them in such desperation and it is a downward spiral into darkness.

Rail, the eleventh day of every month is exactly as meaningless to us as every other day. Do not fall into the trap of believing that to be the case for humans like Tom. The eleventh day of September carries its own special luggage for those in a nation that foolishly calls itself a grouping of states that is united. If rumors in the office are true, we will be spending eternity here in the abyss. If that is the case, then the day of our delight will never arrive. However, we can enjoy the prospect of sucking others into this place of punishment alongside us.

evalS_rekaM:-{((

⸻

From the Chat Room:

FROM: Lilly@firstborn.edu
I had just begun my college days when 9-11 happened. Everything froze that day. Classes all ended. We all sat and watched the events unfold with the crashes being shown on television so many times I can see them clearly even now.

FROM: Jack@west1.net
The same thing happened for me. I remember little of what went on for the rest of the week. I don't think I had ever been afraid since I had been on my own. I

do remember making up a reason to call Mom and Dad to "check on them" to make sure they were all right, but the truth of it is that I was scared stiff about what might happen next. What place was going to get hit next? Who was doing this? Why?

FROM: Thatch@akson.org

Just the opposite was true for me. No, I didn't know who exactly had planned or even pulled the trigger that day, but I was angry. If I could have, I would have killed everyone who could potentially have been involved.

FROM: Harry@humboldt.com

Me too. All I wanted was to get even. Who did those people think they were anyway? They had destroyed so much of value on the east coast. I felt like they should have to pay both financially and physically.

FROM: Lilly@firstborn.edu

I know we are a military powerhouse, but if vengeance is our goal, when will the amount of vengeance we take be sufficient?

FROM: Thatch@akson.org

I suppose you're right about that. After all, aren't we supposed to be doing enough good to be pleasing God? Isn't that what being a Christian is all about?

FROM: Harry@humboldt.com

No. You've got it all wrong. Doing more good or staying away from revenge won't make us better in front of God than the creeps that pulled off these crimes.

FROM: Jack@west1.net

I know we can be terrified or outraged, but none of this discussion sounds right to me. It all appears like we're totally focused on ourselves. That just doesn't jive with everything the Bible says is important to God. His Word speaks of judgment for sure, but God's the one judging for wrongs people commit, not us.

—

Another day, a man stopped Jesus and asked, "Teacher, what good thing must I do to get eternal life?"

Jesus said, "Why do you question me about what's good? God is the One who is good. If you want to enter the life of God, just do what he tells you."

The man asked, "What in particular?"

Jesus said, "Don't murder, don't commit adultery, don't steal, don't lie, honor your father and mother, and love your neighbor as you do yourself."

The young man said, "I've done all that. What's left?"

"If you want to give it all you've got," Jesus replied, "go sell your possessions; give everything to the poor. All your wealth will then be in heaven. Then come follow me."

That was the last thing the young man expected to hear. And so, crestfallen, he walked away. He was holding on tight to a lot of things, and he couldn't bear to let go.

As he watched him go, Jesus told his disciples, "Do you have any idea how difficult it is for the rich to enter God's kingdom? Let me tell you, it's easier to gallop a camel through a needle's eye than for the rich to enter God's kingdom."

The disciples were staggered. "Then who has any chance at all?"

Jesus looked hard at them and said, "No chance at all if you think you can pull it off yourself. Every chance in the world if you trust God to do it."

MATTHEW 19:16–26

Email 38

FROM: evalS_rekaM@loweryet.net
TO: Rail@hellnet.com
Subject: I Get To Got . . . Part 2
Received: 09.13.06

Rail,

Several months ago I communicated with you regarding forgetfulness and the worry, which accompanies it. Your failure to use this tool effectively has been brought to my attention by those further down in the organization to whom I must answer. In considering how I might spur you on in this area, I remembered that when I was still in the field up there like you, the humans had a saying: "There's nothing to fear but fear itself." They had gotten uncomfortably close to the truth. We owe a great deal to the people who unwittingly turned it into almost a cheer. Given enough time and repetition, the effective edge of the phrase has been dulled. Nonetheless, they were uncomfortably close to the truth with this plain saying.

Throughout the centuries numerous types of fear have been useful in keeping people paralyzed in anxiety and doubt:

> Fear that their illness could not be cured.
> Fear that they would never be able to pay their bills.
> Fear that no one would follow as they led.

Worries of this manner can bloom into horror if watered properly. Common bits and pieces out of everyday life constantly prove themselves useful here. So you do not waste my time in asking me to lay out for you how to execute this, listed below is one area of Tom's life where, if done well, fear can play a significant role.

Last week, Tom forgot his promise to get home from work in time to go with C. J. to a ballgame of their younger son Zach. Today the anxiety that he will forget the time and place of the game later tonight has kept him so disoriented at his job all day that his superiors are unhappy and those in our observation center have been laughing themselves silly.

If you can slide it in, let Tom begin constantly reminding himself that their anniversary is next week. Keep him thinking what a cad he would be if he should fail to remember that again this year. If you encourage him to be remembering enough things, it is entirely possible that you may be able to get him forgetting more of them. Then, when he fails to remember one more event, C. J.'s potential explosion at him will add to the reason he has to worry about not blowing it again.

Our generational studies indicate that his desire to improve in this area can be overcome by the fearful apprehension of failure. History is on our side. Simply remind him that he has already forgotten many times. People forget more and more as they get older. Realizing that his forgetfulness will only get worse, Tom has reason both to panic and to excuse himself at the same time. If others do not remember it all, how can it be expected of him? Instead help him keep his own superiority to others in the back of his mind. Since he is better, he should be able to remember more and thus the circle of fears continues.

Habitual forgetfulness is a grand tool. Habit is the key word. Do all you can to feed and water the habit.

evalS_rekaM :-{(

P.S. Remind Tom how many times his repeated efforts to lose weight have failed. Repetition hasn't worked for him. But it can work for you.

—

Responses I received:

FROM: Colin@hobo.com
I related far too well to forgetfulness. My own sense of pride and actual worth has been so tied to my ability to keep a dozen balls in the air at once that as I have forgotten things I have worried about my age.

FROM: Kim@anet.net
My uncle and my grandmother both developed Alzheimer's and, in the end, didn't even know their families at all. Every time something slips my mind, I wonder if I'm going to carry on the family tradition. I hope not.

FROM: Ryan@rpie.com
Both of those are true for me too. But I keep reminding myself that God is bigger than anything I face.

—

". . . Don't be afraid and don't worry. Haven't I always kept you informed, told you what was going on? You're my eyewitnesses: Have you ever come across a God, a real God other than me? There's no Rock like me that I know of."

ISAIAH 44:8

Email 39

FROM: evalS_rekaM@loweryet.net
TO: Rail@hellnet.com
Subject: What, Why, When, How
DATE: 09.18.06

Rail,

Given his tendency to try to work out every detail before deciding anything, soak up Tom's time by repetitively asking questions. How often has he answered the question on the Internet about if it is permissible to download the software not recognized by Microsoft ®? It happens with such regularity that he says yes before he even reads the question. Nonetheless, it consumes his time.

Thus as he walks through a typical day, each time he completes a task, remind him to ask: "What am I supposed to do next? Once that project is completed, what's on deck in my spiritual to do list?"

As he begins to step past that question, raise in his mind the following questions:

When should I begin planning that time I'm going to set aside to grow and mature?

Would it be most productive to tackle each question as it arises, or would it be more useful to tackle them one at a time?

Perhaps it would be most productive if I set aside an entire day for long term planning in this area.

If Tom should consider stepping into that more personal area, it should seem very appropriate for him to then ask why he should invest his energy and effort in growing emotionally, mentally, and even spiritually when no one else around him seems to. Take Dan for instance in the office down the hall. He appears to be the laziest man Tom has even known, incredibly gifted in the area of getting someone else in his department to do what is critical and time consuming. Dan pulls the completed project back in, presents it and takes all the credit for work he did not do unless of course a mistake is made. Then he shifts the blame to the ones who he had been "forced" to work with in that part of the project.

The conclusion Tom is likely to reach leads to my own favorite question in the time consumption arena: Why bother? On occasion when Tom observes or is reminded of an event at all like the one I just described, why should he bother to invest his time in anything? If pursued regularly, such endless repetition of the same questions can push Tom further along the road of chasing what he wants when he wants, or it can send him back to the Merry-Go-Round.

The alternate to the previous question is "Are you sure?" Do not invest any energy worrying about where a string of questions lead. Keep Tom wasting his time asking. Regardless of the answer, encourage him to gather a little more data before he seeks to analyze his findings.

Is this a waste of time? Of course it is. That is the point. Regardless of what he might think about it today, Tom's time is limited. Assist him in wasting as much as possible in asking what is pointless, misguided, unanswerable, or shallow at its best. Do so and you will have stolen time. Steal all you can and he will eventually run out of time.

rekaM_evalS :-{(

—

. . . We've finally figured it out. Our lives get in step with God and all others by letting him set the pace, not by proudly or anxiously trying to run the parade.

And where does that leave our proud Jewish claim of having a corner on God? Also canceled. God is the God of outsider non-Jews as well as insider Jews. How could it be otherwise since there is only one God? God sets right all who welcome his action and enter into it, both those who follow our religious system and those who have never heard of our religion.

But by shifting our focus from what we do to what God does, don't we cancel out all our careful keeping of the rules and ways God commanded? Not at all. What happens, in fact, is that by putting that entire way of life in its proper place, we confirm it.

ROMANS 3:28–31

Email 40

FROM: evalS_rekaM@loweryet.net
TO: Rail@hellnet.com
Subject: Sick Spam
Received: 09.24.06

Rail,

Tragic illness? Cancer? Sickness? Worn out? Sad? Listen to me! You have listened to your human at too high a level for too extended a period of time. Without realizing it, you are slipping into the trap of thinking as he does. If I did not know better, I would say he is flooding your personal emails with spam and infiltrating your personal defenses by use of the multi-attack overflow theory. Regardless of what others may tell you about G_d circling the camp for Tom's protection, illness is a superb time frame in Tom's life for you to attack. Emotional and mental weaknesses are regularly attached to physical battles like cancers. Tom's body is using chemicals that that team of doctors has used in their experiment of "prescribing" to overcome this physical malfunction Tom is experiencing.

Continue to delude Tom into thinking that the letters M.D. Ph.D. or Dr. stand for genuine knowledge on the part of the one prescribing the cures. The next step for you then is to remind him of the number of times such treatments have been insufficient or at best, temporary. Once that is burned into his mind, repeat to him the desperation of depression and lead him to believe that all who even bother to battle cancer are foolish. Regular pop-ups for new medical discoveries can be a help to you at this level if you use them to highlight their need and therefore the fact that after hundreds of years, a total cure for cancer has not been found.

I need not remind you to steer him away from Joshua and Mary. The odds worked against us in their cases and they have found genuine relief in their families. To make matters even worse, they have been duped into believing that J_s_s has been the source of their aid in this matter. Thus they consistently give him credit for the results of pure chance. With their case aside, leading Tom further into depression is no huge step. If you will recall your initial crawling in the darkness training then I will not need to remind you that in so many cases depression is little more than anger, which a person has recognized as improper and therefore swallowed it rather than expressing it. Assist Tom in his desire to be angry but never to let anyone see him as angry.

This man is far too much sold upon the idea that there is a cure for the illness his body faces. Get him past that either through increased suffering or decreased medical assistance and anger will rise, depression will follow. He will blame himself for his own lack of faith in medicine, blame G_d for subjecting him to something which others far worse than himself (by his definition of good and evil) do not have to face. When he tells the medical team of his depression, more chemicals will be sent his way to alleviate his system of depression.

The best part of this is yet to come. The very thought that he should be so weak that he would ever admit needing medicine to handle depression will encourage him to hang his head in dishonor. So guess what? He will not get the prescription filled. At least not right away. Given his personality profile, it is likely that Tom will, instead, seek to manage his feelings by summoning his own strength, and refusing to publicly admit that pain, anger or confusion could be part of his life.

At a bare minimum, sway him to succumb and begin taking the anti-depressant medication. It may or may not assist him physically to do all that is possible to encourage his psychological dependence upon the medicine. Point out the weakness with which he is burdened and the shame which accompanies it and you have increased Tom's willingness to turn anywhere for help even to us. Cancer, and so many other serious illnesses are our friends!

rekaM_evalS :-{(

. . . "Master, my servant is sick. He can't walk. He's in terrible pain."

Jesus said, "I'll come and heal him."

"Oh, no," said the captain. "I don't want to put you to all that trouble. Just give the order and my servant will be fine. I'm a man who takes orders and gives orders. I tell one soldier, 'Go,' and he goes; to another, 'Come,' and he comes; to my slave, 'Do this,' and he does it."

Taken aback, Jesus said, "I've yet to come across this kind of simple trust in Israel, the very people who are supposed to know all about God and how he works. This man is the vanguard of many outsiders who will soon be coming from all directions—streaming in from the east, pouring in from the west, sitting down at God's kingdom banquet alongside Abraham, Isaac, and Jacob. Then those who grew up 'in the faith' but had no faith will find themselves out in the cold, outsiders to grace and wondering what happened."

Then Jesus turned to the captain and said, "Go. What you believed could happen has happened." At that moment his servant became well.

MATTHEW 8:6–13

Email 41

FROM: evalS_rekaM@loweryet.net
TO: Rail@hellnet.com
Subject: Scared to Death?
Received: 10.06.06

Rail,

Death can be particularly handy when we seek to cause dread and yet I caution you to be wary. Many of your predecessors have failed to nurture the fear of death as a means of temptation. Quite often as a man or woman experiences the death of someone they love or that of a good friend, they will express a wish that they themselves could have carried a part of the illness and although they do not say it, thereby spare the life of another. I need not go much further before you realize that such a wish does not come true.

The manner in which you approach the days immediately following such a death will often determine your success or failure with this temptation. In my own decades of experience below you, I have seen hundreds of tools attempted and you will find my own evaluation of the ones I have observed attached below:

1. The belief that "If you had been there more often, they never would have died" is the least useful of these tools.

I find this to be the least useful because if people are given sufficient time, a high percentage of the human creatures eventually judge this as a falsehood and then discard it. Even if it had been possible for them to prevent their loved one falling and breaking bones, their presence could not have postponed a disease. Nor could they have prevented a heart attack in someone else. There is, in fact, nothing they themselves could have done to thwart a multitude of other events that bring life to an end.

2. The belief that if you had taken part of their illness upon yourself, the loved one would not have had to die yet.

While humans say this frequently, they rapidly recognize the impossibility of such a thing and just as quickly discard this idea as well.

3. The belief that G__d is unfair to have this person die when others less important, generous, or loving, live on and flourish.

I have found this to be a tool that works with many, though it carries with it the danger of mentioning G_d by name.

4. One of the most triumphant combinations has been the use of quickly changing the focus, vacillating between weeping and anger, fear and anger, and worry and anger.

My examination of these "tools" continues to be that encouraging people to cling to anger because things have not turned out as they dreamed, helps them lose focus.

Keep them inattentive to anything other than themselves and there is a chance that they will be less attentive to our enemy. You will find that as a primary portion of your job description.

rekaM_evalS :-{(

—

Responses I received:

FROM: Colin@hoho.com
I know I still miss my grandfather. I know he was a great man and that his death was not expected, but it is crazy to say that I should be angry with God for calling his son home. Do I miss him? Sure. Would I like to talk to him and ask his advice? Of course. But would I want him here suffering? No way. The pain is real, but God's promises are far greater.

FROM: Adam@anet.net

I know I can have all kinds of knowledge about death and grief and think that's all that matters. But the real issue for me in terms of dealing with grief is going back to God every time I hurt. God understands how I feel and He is the only one who will ultimately help me in the darkest days.

FROM: Ryan@rpie.com

When my best friend died, my feelings changed every five minutes. But even then, when I didn't know what was coming next or why he had to die in a car wreck, I still knew God was there whether I could see Him or feel Him or not. He never abandons His kids.

God is love. When we take up permanent residence in a life of love, we live in God and God lives in us. This way, love has the run of the house, becomes at home and matures in us, so that we're free of worry on Judgment Day—our standing in the world is identical with Christ's. There is no room in love for fear. Well-formed love banishes fear. Since fear is crippling, a fearful life—fear of death, fear of judgment—is one not yet fully formed in love.

1 JOHN 4:17–18

Email 42

FROM: evalS_rekaM@loweryet.net
TO: Rail@hellnet.com
Subject: Skeptical Thomas
Received: 10.13.07

Rail,

You have done well to keep Tom second-guessing so many portions of his life. If played out properly, his experience today of questioning his supervisor can be promoted as a willingness to think outside the box and real value to his company. We both know however that Tom is genuinely at the point in his life when he has begun to ask whether anything he has ever believed has been right.

A perfect example is his recent checkup at the clinic where his doctor changed Tom's entire group of prescriptions to different medications. Since new drugs have shown themselves more effective, they can reduce some of the parallel problems he has had with his body. Nonetheless, medical changes can be of particular use to you.

Given that he already is wondering if what he has chosen in life is right in general, asking him whether or not he has selected the right doctor, dentist, chiropractor, insurance agent, and even his barber will leave him baffled. The habit of second-guessing everything is a marvelous freeze-frame tool that can summon immense misery for human creatures. Once convinced that choices they made might not have been correct, they become easily befuddled and stop making choices altogether.

In view of the fact that the average person holds numerous careers in a lifetime, this might be a very good spot for you to introduce the question about whether or not he selected the right place to work. Maybe he should start doing a bit of job hunting. Once he begins to walk down that road, helping him consider the wisdom of his lifestyle, the community, his friends, and even his wife. Couldn't he have chosen better? What has he missed out on? Can he do anything about it anymore? The stream of doubts and wondering can be endless.

Let me caution you though, Rail. This is also an especially tender moment for Tom in his willingness to listen to anyone, even our enemy. Keep the string of questions rolling and do not give him time to do anymore than be drowned in all of them. Keep him from asking any real questions and this will be a marvelous time for you, but not for Tom. He can become yet another doubting Thomas.

evalS_ rekaM :-{(

FROM: Colin@hobo.com
I used to think that doubting and wondering only happened to the old. But today I caught myself second-guessing just about every choice I've made in the last year. Then I was reminded that God is greater than anything that comes my way. And He really is in charge all the time. While He never promises I'll always have things like I want, He does promise He will never leave me. And He is far bigger than anything I'll ever face. I wonder how many times I forget that or question whether that's really true.

Later on that day, the disciples had gathered together, but, fearful of the Jews, had locked all the doors in the house. Jesus entered, stood among them, and said, "Peace to you." Then he showed them his hands and side.

The disciples, seeing the Master with their own eyes, were exuberant. Jesus repeated his greeting: "Peace to you. Just as the Father sent me, I send you."

Then he took a deep breath and breathed into them. "Receive the Holy Spirit," he said. "If you forgive someone's sins, they're gone for good. If you don't forgive sins, what are you going to do with them?"

But Thomas, sometimes called the Twin, one of the Twelve,

was not with them when Jesus came. The other disciples told him, "We saw the Master."

But he said, "Unless I see the nail holes in his hands, put my finger in the nail holes, and stick my hand in his side, I won't believe it."

Eight days later, his disciples were again in the room. This time Thomas was with them. Jesus came through the locked doors, stood among them, and said, "Peace to you." Then he focused his attention on Thomas. "Take your finger and examine my hands. Take your hand and stick it in my side. Don't be unbelieving. Believe." Thomas said, "My Master! My God!"

Jesus said, "So, you believe because you've seen with your own eyes. Even better blessings are in store for those who believe without seeing."

JOHN 20:19–29

Email 43

FROM: evalS_rekaM@loweryet.net
TO: Rail@hellnet.com
Subject: Spotlight Shifting
Received: 10.18.06

Rail,

There is great intrinsic value in luring Tom into keeping himself out of trouble by shifting the blame to anybody other than himself. If you need further explanation regarding blame-shifting, refer to the mail you received 03-13-06. Stepping aside from that though, is focus-shifting. This is another marvelous utensil available for you to utilize to keep Tom away from this infernal desire he is developing to get to the real meaning of living.

He is running dangerously close to shifting his focus onto something other than himself. The moment Tom begins to think again about a perspective other than how G_d might choose to have Tom invest his time and abilities, praise Tom that his view is larger, deeper, genuinely more meaningful, and more inclusive than any other viewpoint. Praise him for truly seeing the depth of the issue. After all, whisper to Tom that the last time he elected to use the search engine of www.ask.com to search for "the meaning of life," it pointed him toward nineteen potential answers. Searching via www.microsoft.com it was 4,644, and www.google.com found 169,000,000 potential answers to the question he has begun to ask. Praise him regularly for the supposed "wisdom" of continuously searching for an answer that we labor to make impossible to find.

For Tom to make the next step, his cautiousness dictates that he cannot proceed until he thoroughly examines all possibilities. Only then could he land anywhere. Given the depth of the consequences one suffers if they should trust in the wrong answer, it is terribly unwise of Tom to place his weight on any solution too quickly. So if Tom begins to seriously consider personal achievement as the value with the fewest problems, remind him of the potential value of giving unto those with need, thus tempting him to shift his focus once more and wait to make a move until he has successfully analyzed all possibilities.

Your danger in this is the chance that Tom will begin to consider why he should listen to you and consider your definitions more valid than the other numerous definitions which you have already helped him find as faulty.

At a bare minimum, walk him down this road toward the idea of worshipping the book from which an idea comes rather than the one who might claim to have authored the book. Seriously consider focus-shifting. Then again, you may wish to mull over the value of helping him misunderstand the cost of choosing the wrong idea.

rekaM_evalS :-{(

—

Responses I received:

FROM: Ryan@rpie.com
I was reminded of what a big piece of my generation self-centeredness is. The most recent studies I have seen show that the average guy my age is hit with over 5,000 commercials a day. (www.cbsnews.com/stories/2006/09/17) Is it any wonder that I struggle with anything keeping my attention very long?

FROM: Colin@hobo.com
I know exactly what you mean. I find that I have to go to one special place (whatever it is), turn off my cell phone, not answer any other phones and then talk to & listen to God. Otherwise, there is too much screaming for my attention. If I never listen to Him in the first place, how can I possibly know what He wants me to do?

—

Jesus said, "What a generation! No sense of God! No focus to your lives! How many times do I have to go over these things? How much longer do I have to put up with this? Bring your son here."

LUKE 9:41

Email 44

FROM: evalS_rekaM@loweryet.net
TO: Rail@hellnet.com
Subject: Dreams
Received: 10.24.06

Rail,

"It does not do well to dwell on dreams and forget to live." Professor Dumbledore laid those words upon Harry Potter[7]. While these are merely two characters planted in a merely human movie based upon a merely human book, I cringed as Harry was urged to do more with his life than dream. We have control and influence in myriads of films. I know you have sought to twist and use them to your advantage, but never lose sight of the possibility of Tom turning away from dreams to face reality. If you allow that step and Tom turns away from dreams, you are allowing him to turn his back on far too many potential seductions.

Keep him yoked to his fantasies and it is likely that he will slide into being more greatly dissatisfied with his daily life. Regardless of what he has managed to accomplish or the level he has reached financially or personally, if he is permitted to turn his back on a single want, Tom will be one step closer to genuinely beginning to worship G_d.

If Tom ever turns away from seeking promotions at work, he will be turning away from obsessions that can potentially be tweaked to devour an increasing percentage of his time. Your center of attention in this area needs to be refocused on using every tool at your disposal to consume his family time and certainly time with G_d.

If he should turn his back on fears, you will lose many of the simplest buttons to push to remind him of the frailty, weakness and uselessness of his current personal firewalls. Keep Tom obsessed with fantasies and dreams, especially his own dreams.

evalS_rekaM :-{(

—

Responses I received:

FROM: Ryan@rpie.com
How many of my dreams and goals are really focused exclusively on personal goals and my own desires rather than on serving God? Most of the time, the real danger isn't doing something but why I am doing it.

FROM: Colin@hobo.com
It seems to me that the peril lies in supposing I can meet my own needs.

FROM: Adam@anet.net
It is certainly true that being obsessed with one's own production can be dangerous, but what is so easily overlooked here is that we are not doomed. All dreams aren't traps. We're not automatically tied to dreams. Beyond that, God has planned more than we could ever even guess. His plans are so superior to ours.

—

God can do anything, you know—far more than you could ever imagine or guess or request in your wildest dreams! He does it not by pushing us around but by working within us, his Spirit deeply and gently within us . . .

EPHESIANS 3:20

Email 45

FROM: evalS_rekaM@loweryet.net
TO: Rail@hellnet.com
Subject: Ouija . . . Yes
Received: 10.31.06

Rail,

Oui. Si. Jah. Different groups who allege to have studied the origin of the name for the Ouija board claim it to have come from variations of these human words for "yes." Whether they are right or wrong, we see a parallel in that it does not matter how you entice humans into saying yes to temptation. While some claim the Ouija board can be used to tell the future, others claim it is all a hoax. Some despise it for its ties to the dark side of the universe. Others embrace it for the same reason. One man was recently interviewed on www.latenight. tv.com who said he was certain he had spoken with his great grandfather on several occasions through his piece of board and piece of plastic. A few weeks later, a woman appeared on www.this.morning.near.you.net who denied Ouija to have any valid power. Both people were wrong.

It has never been admitted publicly, but we do not genuinely control much of anything. For centuries our profession has not been built based upon what we create, but on what we steal. We do not have the ability to bring someone back from the dead because we have never been able to bring someone into the world to begin with. Besides, our goal is not to create anything. When nataS led the revolution and seized the power in hell, his motive has always been the destruction of everything held dear to G_d. Success has varied through the centuries, but the goal has been consistent, that of eternal damnation of as many people that we can woo into our camp.

Due to that marching order, the night humans refer to as Halloween has proven itself to be a magnificent annual event when we have been able to dull the senses of people to be vulnerable to our reality and to every temptation. When you consider how to weave this into Tom's life, reflect on the tools that have proven to work in the past. In looking through his records, I have noticed the following:

His desire to be just a bit frightened at times may well be served if you can get him to download the most recent horror flick on the market.

The enjoyment Tom has whenever he frightens others might best be used in luring him into pouring time into a moment of frightening his brother-in-law.

A séance with the fortune teller might continue to keep him confused about what really does lie in the future for him.

Overeating the candy purchased to give to children in the neighborhood when he thinks C. J. isn't watching, can add to their disagreements as well as his obesity.

My point is this, it does not matter if the Ouija board is our invention or not. If you can use it to dull him further to tools you choose to execute in the future, do so immediately. Your success (or lack thereof) on Halloween will serve as a barometer for us below you in evaluating your performance. You do not want to fail. Understood?

rekaM_evalS :-{(

Responses I received:

FROM: Cory@hobo.com
As our first little boy begins to walk, I often wonder what I will tell him when I say he can't be a part of some of the things his friends think is nothing but fun.

FROM: Katie@rpie.com
I know what you mean. Is Trick or Treating really all that bad or is it just one more way I look past what's wrong?

FROM: Adam@anet.net

It strikes me that God made us as creatures that eat. He did that with the first Adam. But to use opportunity eat something tasty as a way to sneak in openness to the occult is nasty.

—

. . . Everything you command is a sure thing, but they harass me with lies. Help! They've pushed and pushed – they never let up—but I haven't relaxed my grip on your counsel. In your great love revive me so I alertly obey your every word.

PSALM 119:86–88

Email 46

FROM: evalS_rekaM@loweryet.net
TO: Rail@hellnet.com
Subject: Brain Tempting
Received: 11.06.06

Rail,

Tom is more highly developed intellectually than the average human creature. That offers you several possibilities and just as many challenges.

First, you should not be surprised when he sees through the simplest of temptations. It is likely that traps you hope Tom will stumble into so you can poison him will become evident to him quickly and he will sidestep them. When that occurs, be sure to point out to him the simplicity of those around him, whether it is real or not.

Second, pride can be conspicuously convenient in drawing Tom further down and further in every day. Help his ego swell and let him be quick to notice the ignorance of other humans around him. Then encourage him to equate plainness on their part with foolishness and weakness and therefore secondary to him.

That brings us to the third potential seduction: weakness. If handled smoothly, Tom can attempt to prove himself as superior to others by recognizing a temptation as a lure toward what he knows is evil and then testing himself to see how close he can get to the edge of it without yielding.

You know yielding to such an enticement is sinful. Tom recognizes that his attraction toward it is immoral. Challenge his superiority by popping up opportunities for him to gauge just how close he can come to crashing before he pulls out of the dive. If he cannot demonstrate his superiority by recognizing a temptation, hovering as closely to it as he can and then moving past it, help Tom begin to question whether he is really as good as he tells everyone else that he is. Is he after all, just fooling himself?

Temptingly Yours,

evalS_rekaM :-{(

—

Responses I received:

FROM: Corey@hobo.com
The image shown here is dramatic. I recognize the half truth described here. I can picture an actor on stage struggling mentally with what no one around him sees. While his friends would describe him as a moral leader of the community, he finds himself staying close to sin just to prove to himself that he's strong enough on his own to walk away when he wants to. It makes me wonder how many times that has been a picture of me.

—

Joseph was a strikingly handsome man. As time went on, his master's wife became infatuated with Joseph and one day said, "Sleep with me."

He wouldn't do it. He said to his master's wife, "Look, with me here, my master doesn't give a second thought to anything that goes on here—he's put me in charge of everything he owns. He treats me as an equal. The only thing he hasn't turned over to me is you. You're his wife, after all! How could I violate his trust and sin against God?"

She pestered him day after day, but he stood his ground. He refused to go to bed with her.

GENESIS 39:6–10

FROM: evalS_rekaM@loweryet.net
TO: Rail@hellnet.com
Subject: PUPS (potentially unwanted programs)
Received: 11.13.06

Rail,

Your assignment this week is to jam spyware into Tom's system. To do so, send email, blatantly calling it an ad, or perhaps letting him know how many million francs, pounds or dollars have been left to him in the will of a woman who died having no children. Her will specified that because she was from America and had always wanted a son named Thomas or Tom, and that all who would step forward who met those qualifications would each receive a minimum of $1,000,000. Regardless of the tool you use to get his attention, be sure to attach the PUPS program to each junk mail you send his way. Given Tom's history, you might want to offer the opportunity to receive a free laptop. All that is required of him to receive it is to provide information regarding his attitude toward numerous foods and then to provide "valuable" market research weekly by responding to our variety of clearly marked PUPS ads.

The amusement for our office in this lies in seeing every place he visits on the Internet since the PUPS will give you an uninterrupted examination of his whereabouts. Add to that the personal information to which you get free access and you will be able to detect his preferences without his permission or even his awareness of your presence. If he should consider adding software which could possibly terminate or limit the avail of PUPS, offer him the free software upgrade of the product he purchases which will block all the most recent spyware, www.easycrown.com which itself terminates all other PUP blockers he might access.

Continuously watching his past choices will aid you as you seek to discern the most effective temptation lure to activate today. Yes, of course we use PUPS spyware on you. Do not bother to try to delete it. It has completely rewired your hard drive, ZIP drive, memory sticks, and you cannot change it. With the hopelessness you are now experiencing yourself, I do hope you begin to see the value of using it against Tom.

evalS_rekaM :-{(

Responses I received:

FROM: Kim@anet.net
I have to admit that there are lots of times that I feel just like this. It often seems pretty hopeless for me to stand up to Satan. After I fail enough times, I begin to wonder if I should even try anymore.

FROM: Ryan@rpie.com
Feeling trapped is one thing. Genuinely being trapped is another. Satan does not hold all power to haunt every moment of our existence the way he claims to load spyware into our computers or our minds. We are not totally weak. No, we can't do things on our own to win. But when we trust Christ, the Holy Spirit is with us 24-7.

Meanwhile, the moment we get tired in the waiting, God's Spirit is right alongside helping us along. If we don't know how or what to pray, it doesn't matter. He does our praying in and for us, making prayer out of our wordless sighs, our aching groans. He knows us far better than we know ourselves, knows our pregnant condition, and keeps us present before God. That's why we can be so sure that every detail in our lives of love for God is worked into something good.

ROMANS 8:26–28

Email 48

FROM: evalS_rekaM@loweryet.net
TO: Rail@hellnet.com
Subject: Giving Thanks For What?
Received: 11.18.06

Rail,

What a joke humans make of Thanksgiving. Get together with a group you do not like, eat more in one meal than many have in a week, and then spend the rest of the day watching a long-standing rivalry that is cleverly marketed as a sports event. I continuously puzzle over what any of that has to do with being thankful. I do find it intriguing though that humans do not see themselves an unthankful, merely deserving however much they have and, perhaps, just a bit more.

To keep Tom's family right where they are, encourage them to begin mentally reviewing what they do not have. Before it even crosses their mind, point out that they should not even bother thinking about their current possessions because so many other people have more than they do. Taking what they have for granted is step one.

The next logical step is for you to frequently remind them that they deserve all they have, and truly a bit more, such as a larger office, a longer boat, or a cabin in a more exclusive area on the lake they love to go to every weekend for two months of the year. Assist Tom's family as often as needed in refocusing on what they do not have. If handled smoothly, you can help Tom be thankful for less every day, bit by bit swallowing the habit of never being thankful for a thing.

Step three, which aided your peers in this regard, is that of the big splash. While in some ways the opposite of desiring more, it has the same effect. Remind Tom that the oldest of the autos they have is a year old and that their house is only 2,600 square feet and is not the newest in the neighborhood. Their neighbor's house next door to them is less than six years old with a larger yard. Therefore Tom's family's dwelling must be far too small. Newer is more desirable. Faster is certainly superior. Why bother with medium or large when extra-large is plainly what he deserves?

Ridiculous as it may appear, each of these maneuvers has worked with other people. Your task is to discern which of them is more easily assimilated into Tom's life. Regardless of which you select, be certain to leave no hint of lasting satisfaction. Thus his appetite for new and faster products will not be quenched and he will continue the pursuit of quantity with the mistaken belief that more of anything is linked to happiness.

rekaM_evalS :-{(

—

Responses I received:

From: Kim@anet.net
My husband showed me the email you sent his way this morning. I've had laryngitis for two weeks now. I used to think I would really like a day off, but since I haven't been able to speak, I couldn't answer the phone, or even speak to anybody. When our two-year old daughter would fall down and cry, I could pick her up, but I couldn't say a word to comfort or encourage her.

Yesterday I started to regain my voice. When we get together with all our family later this week for Thanksgiving, I realize I have a lot to be thankful for just in being able to speak.

—

If you're a hard worker and do a good job, you deserve your pay; we don't call your wages a gift. But if you see that the job is too big for you, that it's something only God can do, and you trust him to do it—you could never do it for yourself no matter how hard and long you worked—well, that trusting-him-to-do-it is what gets you set right with God, by God. Sheer gift.

ROMANS 4:4–5

Email 49

FROM: evalS_rekaM@loweryet.net
TO: Rail@hellnet.com
Subject: War Over Nothing
Received: 11.24.06

Rail,

The verbal battle last night between Tom and his younger son, Zach, can prove to be a splendid beginning for an ongoing war between father and son. If Tom's wife C. J. can be persuaded to take one side or the other, it will be even better. The conflict began as so many do. It is an unspoken war over nothing. Well done!

The report I file later tonight will indicate your involvement and the role you played in encouraging the struggle. In order to be clear, I have attached the file in my database as it currently reads. Feel free to edit the attached file (Undersight Report) and return it to me by 6:06 STC (Satan Time Central) so that I may add to it my final evaluation.

evalS_rekaM :-{(

Undersight Report

Undersight Master: evalS rekaM **Subject:** Rail
Date Submitted: 11.24.06 **Time Submitted:** 06.06.06 STC

On 11.23.06, Rail observed a minor disagreement between T. and his teenaged son, Z. To his credit, he fanned the flame, encouraging neither of them to admit they were wrong or that they had forgotten a single detail. Rail then offered both of them twisted recollections that would make them look better and their relationship always worse.

In general, the battle began thirteen months ago when Z's parents demanded he return home before midnight on the night in question and that if he were unable to arrive by said time he should call home so that T. and spouse C. J. would be assured of Z's safety.

On the night in question, Z. arrived home three hours later than the assigned time. C. J. had not slept. Instead, she worried regarding the safety of Z. and had thought through every hospital within three hours of their home that she could call to inquire regarding safety of their son.

The merit of these events was that Z. had done nothing further than fall asleep at classmate B.'s home after watching a movie. Yet when confronted by anger of parents, his anger blossomed and his attitude was pleasantly painful for both T. and C. J. Responses then chosen by T. were equally filled with anger and accusations.

Reactions by all parties sank lower at that time and were continuously fanned by Rail (due primarily to superior training he had received from immediate supervisor evalS rekaM.) It should also be noted that steps were continuously taken to place each parent in dual positions of reprimanding and accusing Z. and of acting as referee between Z and other parent.

Current plans include extended use of twisting memories to continually divide three humans involved.

Responses I received:

FROM:Ryan@rpie.com
It made me think of our oldest son. I woke him up in the middle of the night to apologize for being such a proud and arrogant dad who acted like I always knew everything and who landed on him so hard the night he got home five minutes too late. It wasn't that he wasn't wrong. I just handled it so arrogantly.

FROM: Cory@hobo.com
Looking back, I wondered how many times I tried to play my parents against

each other. I called Mom today to apologize and you know what she said? Just that she loved me and had long ago decided not to remember whatever I did that was wrong.

FROM: Katie@rpie.com
It's not limited to parents though. As kids we all blow it one way or another. Then we find ways to twist our memories to make us look good.

—

Post this at all the intersections, dear friends: Lead with your ears, follow up with your tongue, and let anger straggle along in the rear. God's righteousness doesn't grow from human anger. So throw all spoiled virtue and cancerous evil in the garbage. In simple humility, let our gardener, God, landscape you with the Word, making a salvation-garden of your life.

JAMES 1:19–21

Email 50

FROM: evalS_rekaM@loweryet.net
TO: Rail@hellnet.com
Subject: King, Queen, Bishop, Knight, Rook, or Pawn
Received: 11-30-06

Rail,

I am intrigued by Tom's fascination with the game of chess. As each piece often plays a significantly different role in the game, it can be used to lead Tom down the path of regular introspection wherein he ponders the role he truly plays in his own life. If on one hand, he is a bishop or knight or rook, he has some power and can push and pull to accomplish many of his own goals. However, if he meets or battles another of similar rank who has just a bit more experience he will be destroyed.

On the other hand, if truth be told shouldn't Tom be the King? Even if he were to begin the game as the least of all pawns, if he plays wisely and everything goes his way, he will be promoted into a position of his own choice so that his king will survive

Thus, in effect, the pawn will begin at the bottom but end on the top. Regardless of the name of the piece Tom selects, lead him to presume that he will be in charge, in effect, the king. Here then is the question to lay before him: If such deep truth is found in the game, how can it be anything but true in real life?

This is something of a unique approach, Rail. Let me know how effective it proves to be.

evalS_rekaM :-{(

Responses I received:

Adam@anet.net
When a team wins a game in the state tournaments, it moves on in the tournaments. Eventually one becomes the champion of it all! If we get persuaded to think that we're that way, how big a step is it to believe there is no king at all, not even God?

Colin@hobo.com
True, but God's Word makes it clear that's not the case. That's a piece of why those scholars in Westminster, when they tried to get a handle on explaining who God is, wrote that he is infinite, eternal, and unchangeable in His being, wisdom, power, holiness, justice, goodness and truth. None of us, promoted or otherwise, can possibly ever measure up to even that minimal explanation of whom God is.

———

Come, let's shout praises to GOD, raise the roof for the Rock who saved us! Let's march into his presence singing praises, lifting the rafters with our hymns! And why? Because GOD is the best, High King over all the gods. In one hand, he holds deep caves and caverns, in the other hand he grasps the high mountains. He made Ocean—he owns it! His hands sculpted the Earth! So come, let us worship: bow before him, on your knees before GOD, who made us! Oh yes, he's our God, and we're the people he pastures, the flocks he feeds.

Drop everything and listen, listen as he speaks . . .

PSALM 95:1–11

Email 51

FROM: evalS_rekaM@loweryet.net
TO: Rail@hellnet.com
Subject: Builder of statues, not lives
Received: 12.01.06

Rail,

Tom claims to love art. Let me recommend you drive numerous advertising flashes his way pointing him to the forty-eight hour builder competition. Once he is at the free art festival, remind him repeatedly of the totally dead state of the wood that artists are carving into statues of their favorite people.

While he contemplates that, ask him if a statue of that sort is really all G_d desires people to be. If that is true, shouldn't Tom begin to agree or at least consider it? Ask him if he wants to be alive or merely a statue.

Doubting G_d's motivation is delightfully deceptive, and probably the reason this is the most used tool with Tom's generation of Americans. Living in his country has a freedom built into it that we despise. Nonetheless, the independence of every citizen is believed to be so valuable that it usually overrides any other values it might claim they hold high.

rekaM_evalS :-{(

FROM: Adam@anet.net

As I was checking my email late last night, the minute I read this I was reminded of God making the first Adam out of not much more than mud. But HE didn't make a statue. He breathed into that pile of mud and gave Adam life. He's not interested in statues. He never has been. He makes us to live walk with Him, to serve Him, and to live with Him. A statue—Hah!

—

. . . God formed Man out of dirt from the ground and blew into his nostrils the breath of life. The Man came alive—a living soul!

GENESIS 2:7

Email 52

FROM: evalS_rekaM@loweryet.net
TO: Rail@hellnet.com
Subject: Lead us, our computer
Received: 12.02.06

Rail,

Every year, Tom's company sends him to Switzerland for the World Economic Forum,[8] where the application of new technology is occasionally praised and raised as potential hope for solving the problems men face. Though we have sought to get Tom's attention in numerous ways, this time he noticed the slogan which we had arranged to have sprayed that day as graffiti on the side of a nearby restaurant: "Lead us Our Computer!" While the wall appeared to have been sprayed by a punk seeking to make a mark in the world, it was done on orders from our office with the hope of planting a seed for Tom to consider later.

His role in the conference was that of taking part in the open discussion regarding the role of AZAZ.2, the most recent software we managed to help his company develop. AZAZ.2 enables corporate computers to evaluate needs and independently change programming in order to facilitate more efficient productions of anything. After the discussion, it was a joy for me to reflect on his desire for something to lead, guide and direct him personally, rather than that direction coming from someone else or from within himself Now is a time he is ripe to pluck him from the tree. He is so starving to be led that he will follow practically anything.

Move quickly. It matters little what you say at this moment. Say something. Feed him a lie, any lie.

rekaM_evalS :-{(

Responses I received:

FROM:Ryan@rpie.com
Each time I re-read this, I am struck again that each one of us goes through such a time in our lives.

FROM: Adam@anet.net
But the point they missed is that we're hungry. It's true we may swallow many lies, yet we're not really starving for any answer. We want the right answer.

FROM: Cory@hobo.com
You're right. Every one of us is starving for what's true. The real question for me was whether I was ready for the ride of my life when God began to change me. Was I ready to live the rest of my life based on the real truth?

—

Those people are on a dark spiral downward. But if you think that leaves you on the high ground where you can point your finger at others, think again. Every time you criticize someone, you condemn yourself. It takes one to know one.

Judgmental criticism of others is a well-known way of escaping detection in your own crimes and misdemeanors. But God isn't so easily diverted. He sees right through all such smoke screens and holds you to what you've done. You didn't think, did you, that just by pointing your finger at others you would distract God from seeing all your misdoings and from coming down on you hard? Or did you think that because he's such a nice God, he'd let you off the hook? Better think this one through from the beginning. God is kind, but he's not soft. In kindness he takes us firmly by the hand and leads us into a radical life-change.

ROMANS 2:1–4

Email 53

FROM: evalS_rekaM@loweryet.net
TO: Rail@hellnet.com
Subject: They are ALL the same
Received: 12.03.06

Rail,

Yes, Tom has a daughter. In fact he has two daughters, Maria and Annie. They are twins in their late twenties who have not been home in over a year. That is why you have never observed them in any part of Tom's life.

While the two daughters claim to be different, they still are identical in appearance, preferences, and taste in clothes. Add to that their level of education and you will see that they have always competed against each other. While Maria has a Bachelor of Science and Masters degree in drama, and Anna has a Bachelor of Arts and her Masters degree in philosophy, they are both currently working towards Ph.D.s in archaeology. Both daughters are married to their high school sweethearts and have two children each, one a boy and the other a girl.

In the same way that Annie and Maria are identical, humans are all really more alike than any would admit. They each strive to be the most significant individuals in human time, crave the same things, long for similar achievements, and even consider many similar things as nuisances. Regardless of how similar they appear physically, we find that it is nearly impossible to know a human creature's special weakness merely by looking at him.

Given that diversity, humans are universally tempted by generic sins. Our Enemy highlighted them in what Tom first learned as the Ten Commandments. Remember those broad areas as you seek to induce Annie and Maria's father to give in and indulge himself in sin. Tom's specialized spiritual weaknesses will become clear to you as you linger near him, but begin tempting him in broad areas, keep careful records of the arenas in which you succeed and moving on to specific temptation zones will come in time.

Your task will become much simpler the sooner you get yourself past the idea of thinking of Tom as one hundred percent different from Bill next door or Sam across the street. Human creatures are really nothing more than identical twin cookies in so many ways. Make use of that similarity. Stop trying to be so creative.

rekaM_evalS :-{(

From the Chat Room:

FROM: Harry@humboldt.com
I have seven brothers and sisters and I can tell you we are all the same in some ways, but every single one of us has our own special strengths and weaknesses.

From: Thatch@akson.org
I only have two brothers, but I agree 100%. Besides, God designed each of us differently on purpose.

God's various gifts are handed out everywhere; but they all originate in God's Spirit. God's various ministries are carried out everywhere; but they all originate in God's Spirit. God's various expressions of power are in action everywhere; but God himself is behind it all. Each person is given something to do that shows who God is: Everyone gets in on it, everyone benefits. All kinds of things are handed out by the Spirit, and to all kinds of people!

The variety is wonderful: wise counsel, clear understanding, simple trust, healing the sick, miraculous acts, proclamation distinguishing between spirits, tongues, interpretation of tongues. All these gifts have a common origin, but are handed out one by one by the one Spirit of God. He decides who gets what, and when.

1 CORINTHIANS 12:4–11

Email 54

FROM: evalS_rekaM@loweryet.net
TO: Rail@hellnet.com
Subject: F.O.G.
Received: 12.04.06

Rail,

F.O.G. is one of our most recent departmental acronyms. It stands for: Forsaking Other Guidelines. It is suggested you upload the software downgrade from www.fogdown/VI6.com. In it, you will find six newly developed tools to reinforce your efforts in keeping Tom befuddled. Regularly list the tools he has attempted to use in the past that did not do what they claimed they would.

The next question of course, is why he should think tools offered by G_d should provide one bit more guidance he can trust than anything else on the market. Being the reader that he is, if he is exposed to numerous free books, CDs and DVDs in the area he is questioning, it is quite likely he will pick them up quickly and be exposed to more perspectives on what the genuine cause of his current challenge might be.

The result, if executed properly, can be one of any of these following consequences:

[F]orsaking all helps offered by others. Do all you can to encourage Tom's lone wolf tendencies. Encourage his false sense of meaningful life which he feels when believes he has accomplished something with no help or assistance by any other creature.

[O]utlandish behavior of his own. Every time Tom does complete anything, remind him that he has earned a pat on the back, which for some means take a day off and go hunting, and for others, it means buying a new car. Even a bowl of ice cream and Tom's favorite pizza can do the trick since his body is developing a problem with diabetes and he is becoming more and more overweight. Because of that, every outlandish fling you can talk him into will merely add to his woe.

[G]rieving at the hopelessness of finding help is the 180° opposite of Forsaking as described above. If you can add just a touch of fear to the inabilities which his physical limits are causing, and remind him of them as frequently as possible each day, you can assist in Tom's shift from worry or fear into bleak and anxious heartache. The marvelous item for us in this is the circle. The more one grieves, the more desperate his situation appears. The more frequently he views any problem as greater than anyone can deal with, the more he will grieve. Keep him in the fog long enough and despair can be the result.

evalS_rekaM :-{(

—

FROM: Ryan@rpie.com
This struck me as how he might have tried to turn Peter away from Jesus while Christ kept him walking step by step on top of the lake and then pulling him out when he was literally in over his head. To claim someone has to stay in the fog is a bold-faced lie. No water is too deep for God to deal with.

—

. . . At about four o'clock in the morning, Jesus came toward them walking on the water. They were scared out of their wits. "A ghost!" they said, crying out in terror. But Jesus was quick to comfort them. "Courage, it's me. Don't be afraid"

Peter, suddenly bold, said, "Master, if it's really you, call me to come to you on the water."

He said, "Come ahead." Jumping out of the boat, Peter walked on the water to Jesus. But when he looked down at the waves churning beneath his feet, he lost his nerve and started to sink. He cried, "Master, save me!"

Jesus didn't hesitate. He reached down and grabbed his hand. Then he said, "Faint-heart, what got into you?"

The two of them climbed into the boat, and the wind died down . . .

MATTHEW 14:25–32

Email 55

FROM: evalS_rekaM@loweryet.net
TO: Rail@hellnet.com
Subject: Explosions on the inside?
Received: 12.05.06

Rail,

Keep interrupting Tom every ten minutes or less during his times of work, when he is at home, at the golf course, and, if possible, even when he sleeps. Our most recent studies indicate that a typical American human will regularly change their focus of attention if given even the most minor push in a different direction.

While media of all types contain such patterns, one place we commonly observe this materializing is television. Moments purchased by commerce and every other year by politicians, tempt people to purchase what they do not have and most likely do not need. This often results in a willingness of the mortal creatures to change channels repeatedly in order to escape the punishment of being exposed to one more attempted sale. Quite often these commercial events are described by Tom and his friends as "one more #!?*¿ commercial." I personally observed Tom change channels over a hundred times during a football game.

If a normal day includes such a frequency of interruptions, it becomes easy to see why outbreaks of frustration (the socially acceptable term for anger) take place. Our records for Tom indicate that a standard day for him includes one such outburst of anger per morning, two additional somewhat stronger outbursts by 4:00 p.m. and at least one stronger and yet swallowed anger toward his supervisor in the office, where he knows that verbalizing his first thoughts will be very likely to cause him an increased number of problems on the job.

There are several opportunities at your disposal to make the most in this part of his emotional life, which I describe below.

Remind Tom as often as possible that his anger is a preexisting condition in his personality. While that phrase could occasionally be accurate regarding medical problems Tom will face later in life, it has nothing whatever to do with his chronic responses to those with whom he works. Nonetheless, if he can be convinced that he cannot help being angry, then the anger must not be his own fault and all those around should accept it and even begin to feel sorry for his inability to control it.

Secondly, the next time Tom allows himself to explode with anger make it clear that the outburst was not his fault, Whisper that another human triggered his anger at work, home, in the store, parking lot, or on the road. They must have been the cause. He could not help it. The other humans present have exposed him to a dreaded flare-up once more. Not only is it their fault, they should be ashamed of themselves for taking advantage of what is clearly a preexisting condition. From what you have reported regarding his past, if you remind Tom of a recent court case where an even remotely similar idea was labeled as true it will become all the more believable to him.

Finally, you might introduce the notion that if a person can explode in anger, vent his system in such a way and then move on, it is really up to other people to "grow up and/or get used to it." If however, another human being has a problem with such action, then it is entirely his or her own problem.

If Tom will not control his emotional hot buttons in any way, push them every time the opportunity arises.

rekaM_evalS :-{(

From the Chat Room:

FROM: Jack@west1.net
I found it disconcerting to see so much of myself described in this. It was as if he was describing me blowing up at my wife again.

FROM: Lilly@firstborn.edu

It's not limited to you men. I have just realized that I tend to point to someone else as the cause of my reaction.

FROM: Jack@west1.net

It strikes me that any of our names could have been inserted there at times. The question for me is what can I do about it?

FROM: Lilly@firstborn.edu

Nothing too large for God to handle if we lay it before him.

—

"This is God's Message, the God who made earth, made it livable and lasting, known everywhere as God: 'Call to me and I will answer you. I'll tell you marvelous and wondrous things that you could never figure out on your own.'"

JEREMIAH 33:2–3

Email 56

FROM: evalS_rekaM@loweryet.net
TO: Rail@hellnet.com
Subject: Postpone it later
Received: 12.06.06

Rail,

With Tom thinking about the comment he overheard this morning regarding the wishes of one of his coworkers that he had made larger investments for retirement earlier, Tom began wondering about an article he read by C. J.'s pastor. Was the preacher correct when he wrote the piece for the website claimed by that disgusting church group about, choosing who you're going to serve and follow?" "Today, make your choice," he had written. "Choose today."

Considering everything that he scans over in the course of a day, those were the only words that stuck with him. You are in grave danger here, Rail. There is a tool that has often been used successfully by your predecessors and one that you must learn to implement, that of procrastination. It carries other names and it commonly referred to as putting it off, adjourning, delaying, holding off, holding up, and laying it over.

Postponement has proven itself useful with Tom in the past, so whenever he begins to consider choices of eternal nature that do not appear advantageous to us, remind him of how long an average person lives in his region. The average person lives for seventy-five years.

Regularly remind Tom that while he is now older than his father was when he died, at fifty years of age, he has yet to reach the average number of years for people in his part of the country. Hint at how he could quite easily live far longer than that because, after all, he is of far better quality than the average person. With much more road ahead, he need not be in any hurry, and thus we can be joyful in his postponement.

If you succeed in keeping his concentration on what is going to happen tomorrow, the likelihood of success increases. If he begins to see the danger of postponing, you might suggest that he must begin to consider its importance when he truly has time enough to give to consider what the topic truly deserves.

rekaM_evalS :-{(

On the road someone asked if he could go along. "I'll go with you, wherever," he said.

Jesus was curt: "Are you ready to rough it? We're not staying in the best inns, you know."

Jesus said to another, "Follow me."

He said, "Certainly, but first excuse me for a couple of days, please. I have to make arrangements for my father's funeral."

Jesus refused. "First things first. Your business is life, not death. And life is urgent: Announce God's kingdom!"

Then another said, "I'm ready to follow you, Master, but first excuse me while I get things straightened out at home."

Jesus said, "No procrastination. No backward looks. You can't put God's kingdom off till tomorrow. Seize the day."

LUKE 9:57–62

Email 57

FROM: evalS_rekaM@loweryet.net
TO: Rail@hellnet.com
Subject: Death in his family...well, almost
Received: 12.07.06

Rail,

You were so close to victory yesterday that it is heartbreaking to be able to taste it and then to have such a victory snatched from one's claw. When Tom's despicable wife, C. J., our long-term enemy was found in that unbelievable automobile accident last night, we all rejoiced that we would finally be rid of her and have greater freedom once her influence had been removed from Tom's life.

As she was traveling to a meeting, she hit black ice. In the first part of a winter storm, her vehicle started slipping, skidding and spinning its way off of the road, into and out of the ditch, sliding all the way out into the field on the side of that rural highway. Then the car turned on its side and slid so that the only way out of the vehicle was to stand on the inside of a window, and try to climb and exit through the passenger door.

Due to the timely reaction of another driver stopping instead of passing by, that miserably helpful ambulance crew removed her and then carried her to the hospital where she was treated and released. Her injuries were relatively minor and so, instead of victory for us, she was released back into the war as one of our sworn enemies.

It is really unfortunate that C. J. lives to continue to tell the story, claiming that she survives due to the display of power and grace of G_d. In spite of that, this string of unplanned events can be used to torment Tom. Remind him repeatedly of his own worthlessness to have such a good wife.

Add to that the torment of "What if?" After all, wouldn't his existence be meaningless if she had died? What else is there that could have any meaning whatsoever if the one he claims to love had died so unexpectedly? If C. J. was all there was to his life, then at its base, he must have no value whatsoever.

Therefore, what sounds humble from him in the beginning can be refocused with a little help from you and if we are lucky, can be tweaked into one more round of hopelessness. The near death of his wife can be used to magnify and enhance his personal worthlessness. If done well, you can use the tiniest tragedies to deflate him a bit further and a bit further until bleak and hollow are all he ever feels.

We do grieve our loss that the accident was not more serious, but do not overlook the ways you can use the shock to our advantage.

evalS_ rekaM :-{(

FROM: Thatch@akson.org
I have often wondered what my life would be like if my parents were to have died while I was still young. It would have been so hard to stand on my own and not ask for their advice.

FROM: Harry@humboldt.com
I hear you there. Even though I so often thought my dad he didn't know what he was talking about, I really did listen to him.

FROM: Thatch@akson.org
Add to that the slap in the face it must be when someone loses a husband or wife they've known for most of their life. No matter how many times they disagree or get on each other's nerves, they have to be lonely.

FROM: Harry@humboldt.com
All that makes me glad I don't have to try to carry those feelings alone. God is there 24/7 – no matter how big the problem or deep the valley.

—

No king succeeds with a big army alone, no warrior wins by brute strength. Horsepower is not the answer; no one gets by on muscle alone.

Watch this: God's eye is on those who respect him, the ones who are looking for his love. He's ready to come to their rescue in bad times; in lean times he keeps body and soul together.

We're depending on GOD; he's everything we need. What's more, our hearts brim with joy since we've taken for our own his holy name. Love us, GOD, with all you've got—that's what we're depending on.

PSALM 33:16–22

Email 58

FROM: evalS_rekaM@loweryet.net
TO: Rail@hellnet.com
Subject: Chronicles or Fairy Tales?
Received: 12.08.06

Rail,

Since Tom seems to insist on making an attempt at understanding the supposed letters from G_d, why not lead him to consider why earlier humans fought so fiercely for 2,000 years? There have been many assertions about who alleged to be victorious over our military headquarters. As you point that out, you will do yourself a favor if you toss in a few names of experts along the way. By using the names of earlier people like Irenaeus, from online sources such as:

1. http://en.wikipedia.org/wiki/Irenaeus,

2. http://www.webcom.com/gnosis/library/advh1.htm, and

3. http://www.1911encyclopedia.org/Irenaeus

you can persuade Tom that you yourself are an expert in the field. Add a few dates and direct his attention to the early battles, not only those focused on dates associated with the stories supposedly about J_s_s, but also the limit of four supposedly reliable books recording His life and deeds:

1. Matthew,
2. Mark,
3. Luke, and
4. John.

Wasn't there after all a gospel according to Thomas? What do the other four have over the one that bears Tom's own name?

The four gospels allegedly contain the same story regarding the one claiming to be the son of G_d. As intellectual and astute as Tom supposes himself to be, he cannot keep his own family history straight more than two generations back. Consider his own family questions below:

Did his great-grandfather move here from Bohemia?

Or was that his great grandmother?

Or was it that side of the family that came from northern Switzerland?

Or was that the Irish side of his father's grandfather?

If Tom gets that befuddled over his own family's past, is it really believable that the one claiming to be the son of G_d could be a descendant of humans on one side of the family? Even if he was, how likely would it be that they could keep track of their family tree? I will not waste your time or mine listing them, yet if Tom insists upon reading it, be sure to highlight the name of Boaz[9] for it was well known that her mother was regularly for sale, if you get my drift.

Consider the possibility of fully recording forty-two generations of family history. Is it conceivable that such a story be anything but a fairy tale? See to it that you highlight this question for Tom more than once. History can be a useful tool as long as you twist it properly and turn him to the portions where a twist of events can assist you in questioning their validity. Wrestle to keep Tom blind when it comes to matters with an otherworldly focus. If you cannot keep him away from the books J_s_s supposedly left behind, at bare minimum keep reminding him of parts of the story where damage control might be possible.

evalS_rekaM :-{(

FROM: Katie@rpie.com
I found myself in a deep conversation yesterday with another teacher in my school. The entire thing revolved around the question of why the Gospel should be limited to four books. As I was driving home last night it struck me that a

much bigger issue is why should we believe the Gospel instead of any of the other ideas out there claiming to be the only true religion?

FROM: Ryan@rpie.com
One of my college profs would have described your discussion as apologetics, defending the Christian faith, but the bottom line is that God is the one who decides what's true. It isn't you and it isn't me. God is a Spirit whose truth never changes. That includes what He tells us about His giving of His Son as an infant at a time we remember each year as Christmas.

—

The family tree of Jesus Christ, David's son, Abraham's son: Abraham had Isaac, Isaac had Jacob, Jacob had Judah & his brothers, Judah had Perez & Zerah (the mother was Tamar), Perez had Hezron, Hezron had Aram, Aram had Amminadab, Amminadab had Nahshon, Nahshon had Salmon, Salmon had Boaz (his mother was Rahab), Boaz had Obed (Ruth was the mother), Obed had Jesse, Jesse had David, & David became king.

David had Solomon (Uriah's wife was the mother), Solomon had Rehoboam, Rehoboam had Abijah, Abijah had Asa, Asa had Jehoshaphat, Jehoshaphat had Joram, Joram had Uzziah, Uzziah had Jotham, Jotham had Ahaz, Ahaz had Hezekiah, Hezekiah had Manasseh, Manasseh had Amon, Amon had Josiah, Josiah had Jehoiachin & his brothers & then the people were taken into the Babylonian exile.

When the Babylonian exile ended, Jehoiachin had Shealtiel, Shealtiel had Zerubbabel, Zerubbabel had Abiud, Abiud had Eliakim, Eliakim had Azor, Azor had Zadok, Zadok had Achim, Achim had Eliud, Eliud had Eleazar, Eleazar had Matthan, Matthan had Jacob, Jacob had Joseph, Mary's husband, the Mary who gave birth to Jesus, the Jesus who was called Christ.

There were fourteen generations from Abraham to David, another fourteen from David to the Babylonian exile & yet another fourteen from the Babylonian exile to Christ.

MATTHEW 1:1–17

Email 59

FROM: evalS_rekaM@loweryet.net
TO: Rail@hellnet.com
Subje ct: Taking a Christmas Break?
Received: 12.09.06

Rail,

I must confess that when your application for vacation time crossed my desk,
I chuckled. You have not been on the field above long enough yet to earn
any vacation time. However, when I saw your requested dates as December
16 through 26, I roared! Christmas-time! I have never issued vacation time
to anyone on the field in the last month of the human calendar. There are far
too many opportunities for the enemy to get his word out on the street in that
season.

Nonetheless, longing for you to be tormented after making such a ludicrous
request, I submitted all the proper e-work and was stunned when your request
was approved. It appears that at least some below you believe that we do not
need to pour ourselves into this holiday time of year. I can only presume this is
because your predecessors have done a remarkable job of shifting the focus
away from the enemy and onto humans desiring and receiving more things.

A prime example of this is the silly story: *How the Grinch Stole Chr___mas,*[10]
where the people shift from wanting more gifts to being together. While it
warms their hearts, that is not the genuine meaning of the holiday. They have
celebrated J_s_s being born for so many years at that time of year, that even I
was astounded how easy it has proven to lead them into shifting their center of
attention from one gift with long-lasting implications to more gifts.

  All that being said, receiving things has been a wonderful tool. If you
simply surf the web for a while, http://forums.macrumors.com/showthread.
php?t=102201 will reveal to you the story of a set of parents who got so
infuriated with the naughtiness of their children that they sold some of their

Christmas presents on eBay™. When that did not seem to do the trick and the kids were still rebellious, the parents threatened to put up the second round of gifts on eBay.

The joy for us is that such actions can help keep humans confused over what their motivation is during this season. Is their focus on giving to others and feeling better about o themselves? Or is it simply on living "better" and therefore receiving more? Add to that the fact that not a single word of the eBay story has to be true, and just that the idea is floating out there on the web is sufficient.

Our private demographic and statistical agency, SatStuRU (Satanic Studies R Us) reported that last year Americans spent $435,600,000 for "the holidays" and gave less to non-profit organizations. While we are pleased by the far lower amounts that were given to charity, we are seeking to nurture the selfish give-to-each-other-so-you-get-more mode. One entire wing of our office is seeking to wipe out the charitable giving altogether with the hopes that the self-centered focus in people will continue to increase.

We do rejoice that their focus is not so much on Christmas as it is on receiving from others and being together one day a year. It is however my regret to inform you that your vacation request has been filed and granted. Let me warn you because insensitive nature of the year does not last. Tom will come to the realization that he does have to pay for the gifts he purchased with the plastic in his wallet and he will go back to work. When that happens, you have to go back to work too.

evalS_ rekaM :-{(

FROM: Thatch@akson.org
My older sister and I were both born on December 25th. True, we both got our own birthday cakes, everybody sang happy birthday to each of us, and we both got presents every year, but as a little guy I felt robbed.

FROM: Harry@humboldt.com
The same thing is true for me, but I have a twin brother. When the day was special for both of us it wasn't really special for me. And I wanted it to be just for me.

FROM: Thatch@akson.org
I wonder if that isn't how Jesus might feel every time we get so caught up in receiving more and being happy about those gifts instead of the gift His Father gave by sending His Son.

FROM: Harry@humboldt.com
It makes me wonder, as kids where did we get the idea that Christmas was all about me?

—

There sheepherders camping in the neighborhood. They had set night watches over their sheep. Suddenly, God's angel stood among them and God's glory blazed around them. They were terrified. The angel said, "Don't be afraid. I'm here to announce a great and joyful event that is meant for everybody, worldwide: A Savior has just been born in David's town, a Savior who is Messiah and Master. This is what you're to look for: a baby wrapped in a blanket and lying in a manger."

At once a huge angelic choir singing God's praises joined the angel:

Glory to God in the heavenly heights,

Peace to all men and women on earth who please him.

As the angel choir withdrew into heaven, the sheepherders talked it over. "Let's get over to Bethlehem as fast as we can and see for ourselves what God has revealed to us." They left, running, and found Mary and Joseph, and the baby lying in the manger. Seeing was believing. They told everyone they met what the angels had said about this child. All who heard the sheepherders were impressed.

Mary kept all these things to herself, holding them dear, deep within herself.

The sheepherders returned and let loose, glorifying and praising God for everything they had heard and seen. It turned out exactly the way they'd been told!

LUKE 2:8–20

Email 60

FROM: evalS_rekaM@loweryet.net
TO: Rail@hellnet.com
Subject: Disaster
Received: 12.10.06

Rail,

Moments ago, Tom was killed in a crash involving his vehicle and several others on I-80 as he was traveling to his work place. The cause of the crash is as yet unclear and meaningless as far as our office is concerned. It remains equally unclear to me regarding his final destination after his last breath. Yet his lack of being here at my disposal leads me to the dreaded report of insufficiency on our part we so often are forced to file. I do report, as do you, to those below me. Therefore I attach the following official notification:

THIS LEVEL OF COMMUNICATION IS HEREBY TERMINATED

OFFICAL FINAL NOTICE: Due to the death of your subject, all earlier emails and communication methods are hereby terminated. You are hereby notified that the doubts, fears, and sins of Tom have been transformed into faith and trust in J_s_s Chr_st alone. While our hope remains that for future efforts, we will be able to lure and lie more skillfully, for the present it is our duty to inform and notify you of the following:

1. Unbreachable firewalls have risen around him.

2. He is beyond all tools available to us at this time.

3. You are required to email all database records of past temptation within the next sixty seconds.

Upon the receipt of these records, you are being reassigned to Tom's youngest son, Zach. But it has been determined through recent studies that email no longer provides the most useful tool for reaching a high percentage of teens. Cell phone messaging is currently more practical and dire for our use since it gives the illusion of speaking to one another without ever allowing humans to hear each other's voices and misunderstanding is dramatically increased. You will be retrained. During that time, your new immediate supervisor, rezinomeD, will educate you regarding the most functional tools in this area.

evalS_rekaM :-{((

—

Two others, both criminals, were taken along with him for execution.

When they got to the place called Skull Hill, they crucified him, along with the criminals, one on his right, and the other on his left.

Jesus prayed, "Father, forgive them; they don't know what they're doing."

Dividing up his clothes, they threw dice for them. The people stood there staring at Jesus, and the ringleaders made faces, taunting, "He saved others. Let's see him save himself! The Messiah of God—ha! The Chosen—ha!"

The soldiers also came up and poked fun at him, making a game of it. They toasted him with sour wine: "So you're King of the Jews! Save yourself!"

Printed over him was a sign: this is the king of the jews.

One of the criminals hanging alongside cursed him: "Some Messiah you are! Save yourself! Save us!"

But the other one made him shut up: "Have you no fear of God? You're getting the same as him. We deserve this, but not him—he did nothing to deserve this."

Then he said, "Jesus, remember me when you enter your kingdom."

He said, "Don't worry, I will. Today you will join me in paradise."

LUKE 23:32–43

Afterword

While I have shared the bits I received by mistake, I did leave one out. It reads as follows:

Email 61

Rail,

Given your constant complaints about system crashes and memory losses, I have downloaded a very simple version of past topics dealt with to assist you on the field daily. To keep it accessible 24/7, I would suggest you download it onto your SDZSP (Schedule-Data-Zip-Stick-Pilot.)

evalS_rekaM :-{(

The list mentioned previously, is on the next pages. Initially, it came encrypted in a way my system could not handle, but for some unknown reason, after defragging my system, the next time I checked my emails, the attachment was entirely readable. After reading it through, I decided to forward it to you. Please note that the Scripture references listed are my own addition.

Last week marked three years that I had owned the same computer. I guess that made it ancient by today's terms so I shouldn't have been surprised when the system crashed. My hard drive was completely fried. Even though my best friend was the most gifted computer genius I've ever seen, he could not do a thing to repair my hard drive or reclaim anything I had stored on it. When he replaced it with a newer, larger, and faster unit with the most recent bells and whistles, I checked my email.

After sorting through a couple hundred pieces, I found several addressed to Rail that were a garbled string of nonsense, either encoded or just garbage with no pattern whatever. From that time to this, I have not received a single piece of which I can make any sense. If I do, be assured I will forward it to you.

Yours in His Grace,
Larry

Date Sent	Satan's Lie	God's Rebuttal
01.06.06	Order and Rank	2 Kings 17:35–37
01.13.06	Knowing What Tom Is Doing	Mark 6:30–32
01.18.06	A Multitude Of Temptation Flops	Matthew 4:8–10
01.24.06	Repetition & Busy-ness as Temptation	2 Corinthians 10:13
02.06.06	E-mailing a Grudge	Matthew 6:11–14
02.13.06	Computer Crash=Life Crash	Matthew 11:27–30
02.18.06	Habitual Crashes	2 Samuel 5:17–20
02.24.06	Short-sighted vs. Long-sighted	Luke 5:22–26
03.06.06	Sick and tired of being sick and tired	2 Corinthians 12:6–10
03.13.06	Using Tom's Work Against Him	Luke 10:38–42
03.18.06	Firewalls	Isaiah 41:9–11
03.24.06	Keep Him Away From Church	Joshua 24:15
03.30.06	Tuning Us In	Job 6:24–25
04.06.06	Fear	Joshua 1:9
04.13.06	The Use of the Polka	Matthew 26:40–41
04.18.06	Blame-shifting	Jonah 3:10, 4:1, 5–10
04.24.06	Trojan Horse	Ephesians 2:7–10
04.30.06	Meaningless Road Signs	Romans 5:17–21
05.06.06	Pre-Modern, Modern, Post-Modern Or What?	Hebrews 12:1–2
05.13.06	Free Vacation!	Luke 12:25–32
05.18.06	Blog this…Blog that…Blog, Blog, Blog	Matthew 7:26–27
05.24.06	I get to got	Romans 2:1–2
05.30.06	The Spotlight—Same Song Next Verse	Job 5:8–13
06.06.06	Mountains and Valleys	Luke 9:28–37
06.13.06	What's his crutch?	Matthew 28:1–8

06.18.06	The MESS of Movies	John 18:33–38
07.06.06	Free Slave	Romans 5:1–5
07.13.06	Arrogant Self-Confidence	Psalm 31:23
07.18.06	Buy now! Tomorrow will be too late!	Hebrews 11:22–24, 29–32, 37–40
07.24.06	Juggling a Wet Fleece	Judges 6:36–40
07.30.06	So Sad…	Psalm 56:1–4
08.06.06	Gatorade, Mountain Dew, or Aquafina	John 4:11–14
08.13.06	Living at the Fair	Isaiah 26:3–4
08.18.06	TIVO or TIME	1 Samuel 2:6–9
08.24.06	The Reflective Restatement of Repetition	Colossians 1:22–23
09.06.06	Phil, the Ruler of Heck	Romans 7:8–13
09.10.06	9-11	Matthew 19:16–26
09.13.06	I Get to Got…Part 2	Isaiah 44:8
09.18.06	What, Why, When, How	Romans 3:28–31
09.24.06	Sick Spam	Matthew 8:6–13
10.06.06	Scared to Death?	1 John 4:16–18
10.13.06	Skeptical Tom	John 20:19–29
10.18.06	Spotlight Shifting	Luke 9:41
10.24.06	Dreams	Ephesians 3:20
10.31.06	Ouija…Yes	Psalm 119:86–88
11.06.06	Brain Tempting	Genesis 39:6–10
11.13.06	PUPS (potentially unwanted programs)	Romans 8:26–28
11.18.06	Giving Thanks For What?	Romans 4:4–6
11.24.06	War Over Nothing	James 1:19–21
11.30.06	King, Queen, Bishop, Knight, Rook or Pawn	Psalm 95:1–7
12.01.06	Builder of statues, not lives	Genesis 2:7
12.02.06	Lead us, our computer	Romans 2:1–4
12.03.06	They are ALL the same	1 Corinthians 12:4–11
12.04.06	F.O.G.	Matthew 14:25–32
12.05.06	Explosions on the inside?	Jeremiah 33:2–3
12.06.06	Postpone it later	Luke 9:57–62
12.07.06	Death in his family…well, almost	Psalm 36:16–22
12.08.06	Chronicles or Fairy Tales	Matthew 1:1–17
12.09.06	Taking a Christmas Break?	Luke 2:8–20
12.10.06	Disaster	Luke 23:36–43

Appendix A

What Was Real And What Was Not?

I quoted many places and people in the pages that you just read. Most of them were fictional. While most of the real people, books, and scenarios received credit in the end notes, to be sure I give credit to all who deserve it, I have also listed below are those who I quoted or mentioned in the order in which they appeared:

Real Websites Cited:

http://www.1911encyclopedia.org/Irenaeus
http://articles.moneycentral.msn.com
http://en.wikipedia.org/wiki/Irenaeus
http://forums.macrumors.com/showthread.php?t=102201
http://www.nytimes.com/2005/10/05/health/05cnd-flu.html
http://www.webcom.com/gnosis/library/advh1.htm
http://www.weforum.org/en/index.htm
http://www.ask.com
http://www.cbsnews.com/stories/2006/09/17
http://www.google.com
http://www.microsoft.com

Fictitious Websites and Individuals Cited:

All people referred to are fictional. Every attempt to make each of these examples appear realistic and distinct has been made and any similarity between a real person and the characters listed is unintentional. All of us will probably relate to at least one of the temptations, shortcomings, or challenges that appear in these scenarios.

AZAZ.2: Software that evaluates and changes every aspect of a company based on its own free will.

FVRU (Free Videos Are Us): Sham web site listing DVDs that highlight hopelessness

Rail (Liar): Devil in training

rekaM evalS (Slave Maker): Rail's overseer/trainer

rezinomeD (Demonizer): Rail's new supervisor after he is retrained dormaR (Ramrod): Overseer of Satanic dept. that creates and distributes the most spy-effective COOKIES

looF rekaM (Fool Maker): Tempter in charge of enticing Tom's boss

Natas: Satan

PUPS: Potentially Unwanted Programs

SatStuRU: Satanic Studies R Us

SDZSP (Schedule-Data-Zip-Stick-Pilot): Memory Stick

STC: Satan Time Central Time Zone

UNDERLAW VI SECTION 9-3: Law requiring notification and warning of demonic failures

University of Ireland Coast: Bogus website Satan uses to plant lies

Undersight Report: Report required of trainer when demon-in-training fails

http://www.easycrown.com: software that disables PUPS-blocking firewalls

http://www.fogdown/VI6.com: Software download from F.O.G. (Forsaking Other Guidelines) designed to discourage humans by listing tools that have not worked in the past.

http://www.latenight.tv.com: Fake website associated with non-existent evening television show

http://www.this.morning.near.you.net: Phony website associated with non-existent morning television show

Notes

1. Lewis, C. S. *The Screwtape Letters* (San Francisco: Harper Collins Publishers Inc., 2001).
2. Throughout this book, each time God's Word is quoted, please note: Peterson, Eugene H., *THE MESSAGE: The Bible in Contemporary Language* (Colorado Springs: NavPress, Copyright © 2002).
3. *Lone Ranger* © Class Media, Inc. 2007.
4. *The Mask of Zorro* © Tristar Pictures, Inc. 1998.
5. *Transformers* © Dreamworks LLC and Paramount Pictures, Inc. 2007.
6. *DILBERT* © Scott Adams/Dist. by United Feature Syndicate, Inc. May 13, 2003.
7. Rowling, J. K. *Harry Potter and the Sorcerer's Stone* (New York: Scholastic Press, 1997) 214.
8. http://www.weforum.org/en/index.htm.
9. Matthew 1:5.
10. Seuss, Dr., *How the Grinch Stole Christmas* (New York: Random House Inc.) 1957.